YOURS TURLY, SHIRLEY

Other books by
ANN M. MARTIN:

Ten Kids, No Pets

Slam Book

Just a Summer Romance

Missing Since Monday

With You and Without You

Me and Katie (the Pest)

Stage Fright

Inside Out

Bummer Summer

ANN M. MARTIN

YOURS TURLY, SHIRLEY

AN
APPLE
PAPERBACK

SCHOLASTIC INC.
New York Toronto London Auckland Sydney

OCHRE PARK IMC

ISBN 0-590-42809-8

Copyright © 1988 by Ann M. Martin. All rights reserved. Published by Scholastic Inc., 730 Broadway, New York, NY 10003, by arrangement with Holiday House, Inc. APPLE PAPERBACKS is a registered trademark of Scholastic Inc.

12 11 10 9 8 7 6 5 4 3   0 1 2 3 4 5/9

Printed in the U.S.A.   40

First Scholastic printing, March 1990

FOR
Uncle Rick, Aunt Merlena,
Carolyn, and Peter

Contents

YOURS TURLY, SHIRLEY

CHAPTER ONE: *September*

BZZZZZ!

Shirley Basini's alarm clock went off and Shirley rolled over, grabbed it, and threw it at the wall. Shirley's clock looked like a baseball and you were *supposed* to throw it at the wall. That was the only way to turn it off.

Shirley loved things like that. She liked jokes and laughing and making people laugh. She had a pearl ring that could squirt out a stream of water when someone leaned over to admire it, and a set of windup chattering teeth, and a pair of green sunglasses a foot wide. Shirley had won the glasses at a carnival. When she wore them, she looked like a fly.

Blam. The clock hit the wall and the buzzing stopped.

"Thank you," murmured Shirley. She buried her head under her pillow. Shirley liked sleeping as much as she liked laughing. But she knew she couldn't go back to sleep that morning.

It was the first day of school. The first day of fourth grade.

"Yuck," said Shirley. Shirley did *not* love school. She hated it. It was her number one hate. Shirley had something called dyslexia. It was a learning disability. Her eyes saw letters and numbers but the letters and numbers got twisted around on the way to her brain. They were turned upside down and downside up, and made into a big jumble. Reading and writing and math were the hardest for Shirley. If Shirley didn't concentrate, concentrate, concentrate, reading English was as difficult as reading Chinese.

Shirley's parents had taken her to a million doctors and clinics before they found out exactly what was wrong. Shirley had thought that was stupid. What was wrong was that she could barely read or write, and math was a mystery to her. Who needed a doctor to tell them that? Any fool could see it.

A more important question was what should be done about it. Everyone seemed to have a different opinion.

One doctor said, "Vitamin therapy. Take plenty of vitamins, especially vitamin A. Good for the eyes."

Another doctor said, "She has dyslexia but she also

has a lazy eye," and made Shirley wear a patch over one eye for a whole year. That was in second grade. It hadn't done any good.

Her teachers all said (and most of the doctors agreed), "Yes, Shirley does have dyslexia. School is difficult for her. But she's a very smart girl. If she'd pay attention and try harder, she could do much better. Maybe as well as Joe."

Joe was Shirley's big brother. He did not have a learning disability. He was nineteen, and *so* smart that a fancy university had practically begged him to come be a student, and then had let him take all their hardest classes. Joe always got As. Straight As.

However, Shirley had a big secret, and she hadn't told it to anybody. Her secret was that she *was* trying. Hard. And look where it was getting her. Nowhere. She had to read baby books and count on her fingers. Furthermore, her third-grade teacher had written something scary on her end-of-the-year report card. She had written that if Shirley didn't do well and make lots and lots of progress in fourth grade, she would have to repeat the grade. *Stay back.*

Oh, boy. That was something Joe had never done. In fact, he had *skipped* fourth grade.

So Shirley was worried. That report card had ruined her whole summer. And now she had to face fourth grade.

Shirley crawled out of bed. She rescued her alarm

clock, which had landed on a pile of dirty clothes, and put on a pair of jeans, her teddy-bear shirt, and her running shoes. Then she stood in front of the mirror and brushed her hair. Shirley's hair was brown. So were her eyes. So were the eyes and hair of Joe and both her parents. But Shirley was the only one in her family who wore her hair in ponytails. She was also the only one who wore glasses. Shirley liked her glasses. She thought they made her look smart.

Shirley tied pink ribbons around her ponytails, put on her squirting pearl ring, and went downstairs.

"Morning," said Joe.

"Morning," said her parents.

"Morning," Shirley replied. For some reason, she was always the last person downstairs. She could never figure it out.

Shirley sat down next to Joe and across from her father. Her mother dished up plates of scrambled eggs, toast, and fruit.

"It's hard to believe school is starting again," said Mrs. Basini as she took her seat.

"I know," Joe replied. "Back to work for everybody."

Shirley grimaced, but all she said was, "I wish you didn't have to go back to college today, Joe. Can't you stick around until tomorrow? Until I see what kind of teacher Mr. Bradley is?"

"I wish I could, kid, but Chris and Henry are picking me up in" (Joe checked his watch) "twenty minutes. Classes start tomorrow."

Shirley nodded.

"It's back to the grindstone for all of us today, peanut," Mr. Basini spoke up. He wiped his mouth on a paper napkin. "My classes start today, too." Shirley's father taught English at DuBarre College in the little New Hampshire town where the Basinis lived.

"And fall hours start at the library today," added Mrs. Basini. "I do hope you'll spend some more time there this year, Shirley," she added. (Shirley scowled.) "The first meeting of the Animal Rescue League will be held this afternoon," Mrs. Basini went on, "and tomorrow the PTA holds a meeting."

Shirley's father had one job. Mrs. Basini had about sixty-eight. Her main job was working part-time in the children's room at the public library. But she also volunteered at the hospital, drove the Meals-on-Wheels van one afternoon each week, and went to almost every meeting of every organization in town. She was only happy if she was busy, busy, busy—helping people and working for "causes."

Unfortunately, one of Mrs. Basini's biggest causes over the past two years had been Shirley and her dyslexia. Mrs. Basini was a great success at everything she did, so she was very disappointed that Shirley wasn't a success. At anything. Worse, Shirley was often a failure. Last year, in third grade, her report card had been a mass of Cs, Ds, and even Fs. Mrs. Basini was *not* happy about that, dyslexia or no dyslexia. Maybe, Shirley thought, fourth grade would be great and she would become a wonderful student, and Mrs. Basini could spend more time with Meals-on-Wheels and less time being upset with Shirley.

But Shirley wasn't very hopeful.

A few minutes later, a horn honked in front of the Basinis' house.

"That's Chris and Henry!" said Joe, jumping up.

The Basinis ran outside and helped Joe load his suitcases and stereo and books and reading lamp and rug and bedspread and pillows into the car. Chris's old Ford looked so loaded down Shirley wasn't sure it would make it to the end of the street, let alone to their school, which was in another state.

"Bye!" Joe called as the car pulled away. "Good luck with Mr. Bradley, Shirley! See you at Thanksgiving!"

The Basinis watched the car until it reached the end of their street. Then Mrs. Basini said, "Better get a move on, Shirley."

It was time to go. Time for fourth grade.

Shirley brushed her teeth, filled her squirting ring with water, and took her lunch from the counter in the kitchen. Since the Basinis had spent so much time saying good-bye to Joe, Mr. Basini drove Shirley to school on his way to DuBarre. Usually, Shirley walked.

Shirley stood outside her classroom. She peeked in the doorway. She was not the last student to arrive at Room 4C. But she wasn't the first, either. About ten other kids were there. And since they were sitting quietly at their desks, Shirley figured Mr. Bradley must be there, too. If he wasn't, the kids would have been running around, talking about summer camp, showing off cuts and bruises, and throwing spitballs or playing with cootie-catchers.

Shirley was disappointed. She had wanted to squirt her pearl ring at Ned Hernandez. Oh, well. Maybe later in the day.

Shirley took a deep breath. She patted her pony-tails and tried to tuck in her teddy-bear shirt. Then she stepped into Room 4C.

Mr. Bradley was there, all right. He was sitting on his desk (not *at* it, *on* it). The desk was next to a wall which Shirley hadn't been able to see from the door-way. "Good morning," said Mr. Bradley pleasantly. "And you are—?"

Shirley knew she was supposed to say, "Shirley Basini," but she couldn't pass up the opportunity for a good laugh. She just couldn't. Her classmates ex-pected her to make them laugh. And, when Shirley thought about it, that was the only thing she did even halfway well in school. Make the kids laugh.

"I'm fine, thanks, and you?" said Shirley.

Her classmates giggled, but very quietly. Even though Mr. Bradley was sitting on his desk, they didn't know if he was the kind of teacher who liked jokes.

Mr. Bradley smiled. "Couldn't be better," he replied.

Shirley let out a breath. Maybe Mr. Bradley would be okay after all.

"Your name, please?" Mr. Bradley went on.

"Shirley Basini."

"Okay, Shirley Basini. Your desk is right over there. Would you please take a seat?"

"Take a seat? Sure." Shirley set her lunch box on her desk. Then she picked up her chair. "Where would you like me to take it?" she asked politely.

She was pleased to hear more laughter, but Mr. Bradley said, "I meant, *sit on it*." He didn't sound so pleasant anymore.

Shirley sat.

She watched as the rest of her classmates entered the room. Mr. Bradley greeted them. Each time he said, "And you are—?" the student answered with his or her name. No one else said, "Fine, thanks, and you?" Shirley felt quite happy. At least she was off to a good start with the other kids.

The bell rang. Mr. Bradley looked around Room 4C with satisfaction. Every seat was filled. "Shirley," he said, "would you please hop up and close the door?"

Shirley grinned. What an opportunity. "Okay," she replied. She stood up, lifted one foot in the air, and hopped over to the door. She closed the door and hopped back to her desk.

The kids laughed.

Mr. Bradley smiled. "Ah. I see we have a comedienne. Shirley, why don't you come up here and give us your whole routine right now? You could get it out of the way, and I'm sure the class would enjoy it. It would be a pleasant start to the new school year."

Her routine? Shirley didn't have a routine—exactly. She slid down in her seat, her face reddening. "Uh, no thanks," she told her teacher. "Maybe later."

"Fine," replied Mr. Bradley. "No more funny business, then."

Shirley nodded.

Mr. Bradley began the day. He led Shirley's class in the Pledge of Allegiance. He explained his classroom rules. He assigned cubbies where coats and lunches could be kept. He handed out science books and social studies books.

Yuck, thought Shirley.

Finally, Mr. Bradley stood in front of 4C with a stack of papers. "I am now going to pass out—"

Shirley jumped up from her chair. "Help him!" she cried. "He's going to pass out! Get the smelling salts! Call the nurse!"

"That will be quite enough, Shirley," said Mr. Bradley, but the class didn't hear him. Everyone was laughing too hard. "That will be *quite enough*, Shirley," Mr. Bradley repeated, more loudly.

It wasn't necessary for him to repeat it. Shirley was already sitting down again.

Mr. Bradley handed out the papers.

Shirley looked down at hers and felt her stomach flip-flop. *A test*. A test on the first day of school.

"This is not a test," said Mr. Bradley. "It's an evaluation. It will help me find out what your reading, math, and spelling skills are. I've looked at your records from last year, but now I want to see your actual work. You will not be graded, so don't worry about this. Just try to relax and do your best. You may begin."

Shirley tried to read the first word on the page. The letters swam before her eyes. MANE? Oh, no. Of course. NAME. Shirley wrote her name on the line. Then she moved on to the rest of the page. It was filled with problems and questions. Shirley read the first one slowly.

If Mary has four bags with three apples in each, and John has two bags with four apples in each, how many apples do Mary and John have together?

Numbers, numbers, numbers. Shirley felt confused with all those fours and threes and twos in her brain. She did what her teachers had always told her to do. She concentrated. Hard. It didn't help. Four, three, two. Three, four, two. Shirley wanted more than anything to find the right answer for Mr. Bradley, but she was running out of time. She couldn't take this long on every problem. Should she skip it? No, she couldn't skip the very first one. She had to write down some answer. She thought and thought. At last she wrote, THEY HAV a lot BUT I THINK Mary Has mor SH9 sHolD giv Some To Jon or else she will Be a pig.

When Mr. Bradley finally collected the papers, Shirley let out a huge sigh. She knew she'd done badly, as usual. But she didn't know how badly until after lunch. Mr. Bradley must have looked at the evaluations as soon as Shirley and her classmates went to the cafeteria. Right after recess he assigned spelling. groups, reading groups, and math groups. He put everyone but Shirley into a group. He handed out workbooks and readers, and gave each group an assignment. Then he called Shirley to his desk.

I'm in trouble *already*? thought Shirley.

"Shirley," Mr. Bradley whispered.

"Yes?"

"I've looked at your evaluation. And before school

started, I talked to your third-grade teacher."

"You did?" said Shirley in a small voice.

"Yes. And I'm aware of the trouble you've been having. I want you to know that I'll give you plenty of extra help this year. I'll do anything to keep you from staying back. But you have to help me. We both have to work hard. If you like, you could even get some extra help in the Resource Room."

"The Resource Room! But that's for retards!"

"Shirley," said Mr. Bradley, "in the first place, that's not true. And in the second place, 'retards' is not a very nice word."

"Sorry."

"That's okay. All right. We'll forget about the Resource Room for now. But you have to agree to work with me, and to work hard. Is that a deal?"

"Deal," said Shirley, feeling relieved about the Resource Room.

"Good. Now you may not like everything I decide to do, but I'm counting on you to cooperate."

Mr. Bradley was right. Shirley certainly didn't like everything he did. For starters she wound up in the worst, most babyish spelling and math groups of all. (No matter what the teacher named the groups, you could always tell which was worst and which was best.) But the most horrible thing was that Shirley wound up in a reading group all by her*self*. And Mr.

Bradley had to leave the room to find a special second-grade reader for her.

Shirley hung her head. But while her teacher was gone, she got an idea. "Hey, Ned!" she called.

Ned Hernandez looked up from a piece of paper on which he was drawing two spaceships that were crashing in a fiery explosion. In third grade, Shirley had liked Ned. Sort of.

"Yeah?" said Ned.

Shirley stood up. "Look at the ring my parents gave me for my birthday. It's a real pearl. Isn't it pretty?"

She held it out.

Ned leaned over to look at it. "How come they let you wear a real pearl to school?" he asked.

Shirley didn't answer. *Squish.* She squeezed the little rubber ball that was hidden in her hand. Water sprayed out of the pearl and into Ned's face.

"Hey!" he cried.

Shirley thought he was going to get angry. Instead he said, "Cool. Can I see it?"

Shirley took her ring off. She handed it around. Everyone was very impressed. They were so impressed that they hardly paid any attention when Mr. Bradley returned with the second-grade reading book for Shirley.

A little while later, the bell rang and Shirley

breathed a sigh of relief. Somehow, she had squeaked through the first day of school.

When Shirley got home that afternoon, she found a surprise. Her mother was there. So was her father. Mr. Basini was hardly ever at home when school let out.

Mrs. Basini greeted Shirley with a big hug. "We have wonderful news for you," she said. "You'll never guess."

"Tell me, then," said Shirley. "What?" She was relieved that her mother hadn't asked about school. She always asked how it had gone, and would have been terribly disappointed to hear about her evaluations and the second-grade reader.

"You are going to be a big sister. You're going to have a brother!"

Shirley was speechless.

"Isn't that wonderful?" said her father.

Shirley found her voice. "You're pregnant, Mom?" she asked incredulously. Mrs. Basini was older than the mothers of most of Shirley's friends.

"No," said her mother. "We've adopted a child. Last year your father and I decided that we could help out by giving a home to a child who really needs one."

Ah, thought Shirley. Another one of her mother's causes.

"So we applied to adopt a Vietnamese child. And the agency called us today. A child is available. He's three years old. And he'll be ours next month, on October fifteenth."

"What do you think, peanut?" asked Mr. Basini.

"I think," replied Shirley, a smile spreading across her face, "that it's great! I mean, good. I mean, okay. I mean, I'm not sure." Her smile faded away.

"That's all right," said Mrs. Basini, straightening Shirley's untidy ponytails. "We all have to get used to the idea. Joe, too. He doesn't even know yet. Would you like to call and give him the news?"

"I guess so. I'll do it later."

Shirley went to her room to think. She, Shirley Taylor Basini, was going to be a big sister. She hoped she was ready for the job.

CHAPTER TWO: *October*

"Mom, where are the clean pillowcases?"

"In the laundry room. Shirley, what did you do with that baby minder your father bought on Saturday?"

"I put it on the shelf in Joe's closet. . . . You know, I don't think we have enough new clothes. You only bought three shirts."

"He's coming with some clothes of his own, hon."

It was Wednesday, October twelfth. In just three days, Shirley's new little brother would arrive. Shirley and her mother were very busy. They were fixing up half of Joe's room for a three-year-old boy. (This was a terrific project, since it kept Mrs. Basini's mind off of Shirley's schoolwork.) On one side of the room was Joe's bed, his dresser with his soccer trophies, a bookcase, and his computer. On the other side was a new bed. It was covered with a bedspread that had bright red cars and trucks printed on it. Nearby was a chest filled with Shirley's old toys and puzzles and stuffed animals. On a white bureau stood a teddy-bear lamp.

"This room looks like What's Wrong with This Picture?" said Shirley, entering with the pillowcases.

Mrs. Basini laughed. "Joe will die when he sees it. But he's not home very often anymore, so I don't think he'll mind much."

Shirley thought of her good-natured big brother. She knew he wouldn't mind at all.

The phone rang then, and Shirley dropped a pile of neatly folded pillowcases on the floor. "I'll get it!" she yelled.

"Shir-*ley*," her mother admonished her, pointing to the floor. She shook her head at Shirley's carelessness.

"Sorry," said Shirley, tripping over them as she ran out of the room. She picked up the phone in the hall-way. "Hello?" she said breathlessly. (Shirley just loved to answer the phone. You never knew who might be on the other end. Maybe it was Joe . . . or a guy saying she'd won a million dollars and a clock radio in a contest.)

Shirley listened for a moment. Then she rested the receiver on the table. "Mom!" she called. "It's the adoption agency. The lady says it's important."

Mrs. Basini bustled out of the bedroom. "Yes?" she said into the receiver. "Mrs. Cooley? . . . Oh, I *see*. . . . Mm-hmm, mm-hmm."

Shirley leaned against the doorjamb and listened to her mother's end of the conversation. She wished Mrs. Basini would say something more than "I see" and "Mm-hmm."

At last she did. "*Eight* years old?! . . . Well, no, of course not. I don't see how we can. I mean, after all, we just wanted another child. But we did think it would be nice to have a younger one. . . . No, no. Don't worry. I'll have to speak to my husband, of course, but I'm sure he'll feel the same way. . . . Yes. . . . Yes. . . . All right. We'll be at the airport on Saturday." Mrs. Basini hung up the phone, frowning.

"What is it?" asked Shirley. She was dying of curiosity.

Mrs. Basini walked slowly into the room and sat on Joe's bed. "There's been a mix-up," she said, rubbing her forehead.

"A mix-up?" Shirley repeated. She began to feel funny, the way she did when a teacher placed a surprise quiz paper in front of her.

"Yes," replied Mrs. Basini. "We're not getting a three-year-old boy on Saturday. We're getting an eight-year-old girl."

"A *girl*? An *eight*-year-old girl? That's almost my age!"

"I know, I know. It isn't at all what we expected. But how can we say no? She needs a home, too. And that was what your father and I wanted to do—give a home to a child who needs one. And here *we* are, and there *she* is. . . ."

That night Mr. and Mrs. Basini talked for a long time. Shirley wasn't at all surprised when they told her at breakfast the next morning that she was going to be big sister to a girl, not a boy.

But she *was* surprised when her father said, "Of course, we'll have to make some fast changes. She'll have to share your room, Shirley, not Joe's."

"*My* room! How come?"

"Because Joe's a boy," her mother said. "He isn't home much, but he is home during the summer and on vacations. And he can't be expected to share a room with an eight-year-old girl."

"Couldn't he sleep on the couch or something?" asked Shirley.

"Not for an entire summer, honey," said her mother. "That's not fair. We don't want to take his room away from him."

"You're taking mine away," said Shirley grouchily.

"Not really," Mr. Basini told her. "We're just asking you to share it."

Shirley nodded. Her father, it seemed, could make anything seem better.

* * *

The preparations for Shirley's sister began.

Mrs. Basini put the new baby minder out in the garage. They wouldn't need the intercom to listen in on an eight-year-old. Some of the baby toys were put in the garage, too.

"What's her name, anyway?" Shirley asked her father that evening as they moved the lamp and dresser and bed out of Joe's room and into hers.

"Oh, it's entirely unpronounceable. I couldn't begin to repeat what Mrs. Cooley told your mother."

Shirley smiled. She liked the way her father would come right out and admit when he couldn't do something. He didn't try to be perfect, the way her mother did.

"Will her last name be Basini?" asked Shirley thoughtfully, as she smoothed out the car-and-truck bedspread.

"Yes," replied her father. "And I think we'll give her a new first name. Would you like to help pick out a name?"

"Sure!" replied Shirley.

When she went to bed later that evening, Shirley lay against her pillow and looked at the shadows in the room. There were a lot more shadows than there had been the night before. Her room was very crowded—two dressers, two beds, two night tables, plus Shirley's desk and chair.

All day Shirley had wondered what having a sister

would be like. She was not thrilled about sharing her room, but she had decided that a sister might not be so bad. For one thing, *her* sister wouldn't be able to speak English. Shirley hoped that she and her parents would be so busy trying to teach her English that her mother wouldn't have time to worry about things like Shirley's second-grade reading book. Or the spelling test that had been returned to her that morning with nine out of ten wrong. And if Shirley could teach her sister English, maybe her mother would be proud of her for once.

Shirley was looking forward to teaching her sister all sorts of things. She bet the girl wouldn't know anything about TV or stuffed animals or video games. Who knew what her orphanage in Vietnam had been like? Maybe she'd never gone to school or sat in front of a mirror and played beauty parlor or eaten a chocolate bar or a slice of pizza.

Shirley's excitement was growing. For once, someone needed her. Shirley could be the leader, the teacher, the explainer. She couldn't wait for Saturday.

Shirley fell asleep thinking of names for her sister. Ellen? No. Erica? No. Tammy, Amelia, Nancy, Jackie, Rachel, Leah, Lynn . . .

Oh, Saturday, please hurry up!

Saturday didn't hurry, but it did arrive.

By the time the Basinis left for the airport, they had

decided on a name for Shirley's sister—Jacqueline
Sara Basini. They would call her Jackie. It had taken
a long time to choose a name, but everyone had liked
Jacqueline Sara. Shirley had even phoned Joe at college to make sure he liked the name. He did.

Late Saturday afternoon, Shirley and her parents
arrived at the big airport in Boston, Massachusetts.
They were going to meet a flight from California.

"Twelve Vietnamese children will be on the
plane," Mr. Basini explained to Shirley as they waited
at the gate. "They've been adopted by families in
New England."

Shirley looked around at the people in the waiting
area. Most of them appeared excited. She saw three
couples with no other children, and one family that
already included six children—black, white, and
brown.

"How come the flight is from California?" Shirley
wanted to know.

"Because the most direct route from Vietnam to the
United States is east," her father explained patiently,
"and the plane reaches California first. Jackie and the
other children changed planes there. The kids will be
exhausted by the time they reach Boston. They will
have been traveling for hours and hours and hours."

"I hope Jackie got on the right plane in California,"
said Shirley nervously.

"Oh, don't worry," said her mother. "Four people

from the adoption agency are traveling with them. They're well taken care of."

"Hey," cried Shirley, "look at that!"

Two men and two women with big cameras had rushed into the waiting area. They were followed by a crew from a TV station. Reporters began interviewing the families who were waiting for the flight.

"Wow," exclaimed Shirley softly, "I guess this is a pretty big deal."

"It's not every day that a group of orphans from halfway around the world arrives in Boston to go to new homes," a newspaper reporter told Shirley. "What's your name?"

"Shirley Basini," Shirley replied proudly. "I'm waiting for my new sister. Her name is going to be Jacqueline Sara Basini. I've never had a sister."

"And are these your parents?" asked the reporter.

Shirley nodded.

Her parents introduced themselves and answered the reporter's questions about how they had found Jackie and how the adoption had been arranged. Then a woman with a camera took a picture of the Basinis.

A tinny voice came over the loudspeaker. "Announcing flight three-oh-eight from Los Angeles," it said. "Three-oh-eight from Los Angeles."

"That's it! That's Jackie's plane!" cried Mrs. Basini.

Shirley and her parents jumped up and joined the crowd of people at the railing near the flight gate.

People from the plane began to enter the waiting area. First came a businessman with his briefcase. An old man and an old woman followed him slowly and waved to someone, their faces breaking into smiles. A mother and father with two children came out. And then an American woman with an Asian baby in her arms walked into the waiting area. A sign saying PE-TERSON was hanging from her arm.

"Here we are!" shouted two excited voices.

Shirley turned around to look, but her father tugged at her sleeve. "I think Jackie's here," he said softly.

Shirley turned back to the gate. Emerging into the waiting room in a frightened huddle were five Asian children—two boys and three girls—and another American woman. Each child carried a paper bag. On the shirt of one of the girls was pinned a big tag that said BASINI.

Shirley and her parents rushed over to the girl.

"We're the Basinis!" Shirley's mother told the woman from the adoption agency. And then she gathered the girl into her arms.

Jackie began to cry. So did Shirley's mother. So did Shirley's father. So did Shirley. A reporter snapped their picture.

"This is your sister," Mrs. Basini told Jackie. She pulled Shirley close, and Shirley took Jackie's hand.

Nobody knew whether Jackie understood what was being said, but it didn't matter.

There were more hugs and tears and smiles. Mr. Basini spoke to the woman from the agency. Everywhere, families were greeting their new children. Flashbulbs went off. A TV camera zoomed in on Shirley and Jackie. Shirley smiled and waved. "This is my sister," she announced.

Jackie was tiny. Even though she was just a year younger than Shirley she was a whole head shorter. And she looked fragile, as if a gust of wind could blow her to the ground. She gazed at Shirley out of dark almond-shaped eyes under a fringe of choppy black hair.

"We," said Shirley to Jackie, "are going to have to do something about your hair."

"Hair?" repeated Jackie, and touched her head.

"You speak English?" said Shirley disbelievingly.

"Engrish," said Jackie.

"What's in your bag?" asked Shirley. She pointed to Jackie's paper bag, and Jackie held it out to her. Shirley peeked inside. She saw an old shirt, a pair of socks, and a faded dress. Were they Jackie's only belongings?

A reporter moved in for another picture and Jackie pressed her face against Shirley's shoulder and began to cry again.

"No more pictures," Shirley told the man importantly. "She's shy."

"And tired," added Mrs. Basini.

"And confused," added Mr. Basini. "Come on. It's time to go home."

Shirley would never forget her first night with Jackie. She could only describe it as surprising. She was surprised that Jackie knew a little English. Jackie had learned it in the orphanage—not much, but enough to communicate with the Basinis when she was hungry or had to use the bathroom, and enough to point to some things and name them.

She's like a little kid who's just starting to talk, thought Shirley.

Shirley was surprised again when the Basinis reached their house and sat down to their first meal with Jackie. Jackie ate like a bird. When anyone offered her second helpings, she said no—very politely. But after dinner she managed to hide a pile of food in a napkin, and later take it to bed with her. Shirley found it when she realized that her room smelled like peas and mashed potatoes.

"Why would she hide food?" she asked her father.

"She's probably never had enough to eat," he replied slowly. "She must think she has to hoard food when there's extra."

Shirley's last surprise was the way Jackie began to

cling to her that evening. She stuck to Shirley like glue until bedtime, and barely spoke to Mr. and Mrs. Basini.

"I think she feels more comfortable with you," said Mrs. Basini. "You're close to her age. Your father and I must look like big, scary people to her."

Shirley laughed.

That night, after the lights were out, an exhausted Jackie crawled out of her new bed with the car-and-truck spread on it and into Shirley's bed. Shirley had never felt more important. She hoped she could do a good job of being the big sister Jackie needed.

On Monday, Shirley went to school, but Jackie wasn't ready to go. Instead, Mrs. Basini took Jackie to the doctor and the dentist for checkups, to the department store for more clothes, and to a special teacher to see what should be done about Jackie's English and when she would be ready for school.

Shirley was a celebrity in Mr. Bradley's room. Almost everyone had seen her on the news on Saturday night. During social studies, Mr. Bradley even canceled the usual textbook assignment and called Shirley to the front of the room.

"Why don't you talk to the class about adopting a foreign child?" he said.

Shirley's eyes widened. "*Me?*" she replied.

Mr. Bradley smiled. "You're the only one I know

who got a Vietnamese sister over the weekend."

So Shirley told her family's story. Later, her class-mates asked questions. Shirley answered all of them. She felt like the teacher instead of just a student. She was almost able to forget that she had flunked a math test on Friday.

One week later, Jackie started school. Even though she was eight years old, she was put in a first-grade classroom.

"Just until her English improves," said Mrs. Basini. "And until she learns how to read and write in Eng-lish."

Poor Jackie, thought Shirley. That could take for-ever. Reading and writing were *hard*, even when you were paying attention, which was what Shirley was trying to do.

As it turned out, neither reading nor writing was Jackie's biggest problem. Her biggest problem was being afraid. Mrs. Basini had to stay with Jackie for her entire first day in school and half of her second. On the third day, Mrs. Basini left, but Shirley was called out of Mr. Bradley's room twice to help Jackie.

"Everything is new for her," Shirley told Jackie's teacher. "Call me any time she needs help."

The teacher called her a lot at first, and then less and less often.

By Halloween, Jackie knew how to say one

hundred English words. (Shirley had been keeping track of them on a list that she taped to the wall in their bedroom.) Jackie had walked home from school by herself three times. She had learned how to answer the telephone. She liked TV, and she loved to look at picture books.

Shirley tried to explain Halloween to Jackie. She told her about witches and goblins and ghosts. Jackie looked blank. Finally, Shirley colored a huge picture of kids trick or treating on Halloween night. She put a full yellow moon in the sky with a dark cloud scudding in front of it. She added a witch on a broomstick flying near the moon. She put a black cat in the bare branches of a twisted, evil-looking tree. And down below, she drew masked trick or treaters going from door to door in their costumes.

Jackie loved the picture.

Then Mr. Bradley announced a Halloween poster contest in Shirley's class. Shirley entered her picture.

She won first place!

What a way to end October, thought Shirley. She felt happier than she had felt in a long, long time. Her mother was happy, too. Finally, Shirley had succeeded at *some*thing.

CHAPTER THREE: *November*

Nobody was prouder than Shirley of the progress Jackie was making. Every time Jackie learned a new word or came home from school carrying a paper with a foil star on the top, Shirley beamed. After all, she was Jackie's personal, private, and very special tutor. She had taught her about Halloween and helped her to make a ghost costume. She had made flash cards of first-grade words for her. And she had run down to Jackie's classroom to rescue her every time she needed rescuing.

By the middle of November, when Jackie had been Shirley's sister for a month, Jackie's teacher had stopped calling Shirley for help.

"Jackie's doing beautifully," she told Shirley one afternoon when Shirley stopped by to walk Jackie home.

Jackie beamed. She understood exactly what "She's doing beautifully" meant.

Shirley beamed, too.

As they walked away from school that day, Shirley said to Jackie, "You know, the next step is for you to make friends."

"Friends?" repeated Jackie, looking up at Shirley.

"Yeah," replied Shirley. "You need a few. Everyone does."

Shirley didn't have a best friend, but she was friendly with all the students in Mr. Bradley's class, even Ned Hernandez. And she knew most of the kids in her neighborhood. Jackie, on the other hand, just had Shirley. She stuck with her every possible moment. She stuck with her so much, in fact, that Shirley herself hadn't invited a friend over since Jackie had arrived. Mrs. Basini had tried inviting one or two of Jackie's first-grade classmates over, but Jackie had been too new then. She hadn't known enough English. The afternoons had been disasters. "We'll just take this slowly," Mrs. Basini had said. But she'd looked a bit annoyed.

Now it's time to do something, Shirley thought. Jackie is ready.

And on the very next Saturday, she did do something.

"Jackie," she said, "today we are going to have a friend over for you."

"A friend to pray?" said Jackie, looking worried.

"To *play*," replied Shirley firmly. "It'll be fun." She took Jackie by the hand. "I promise."

Shirley picked up the phone and dialed Erin Bayard's house. "Hi, Erin," she said, "it's me, Shirley. I was wondering if Sessie would like to come over to play with Jackie today. . . . Oh. . . . Oh. . . . Oh, yeah? Well, that would be fine. Great, in fact. Do you want to come, too? We could bake cookies or something. . . . Oh. Okay, no problem. . . . Yeah, we'll look for Sessie and Joan in a few minutes. Thanks. . . . Okay, bye."

Shirley hung up the phone and turned to Jackie. She felt more grown-up and motherly than ever. "Guess what?" she said.

By then, Jackie knew enough to say, "What?"

"Two girls are going to come over to play with you. Their names are Sessie and Joan."

"What do we pray?" asked Jackie.

"Don't worry so much," Shirley told her.

Shirley had chosen Sessie Bayard (whose real name was Susan) because she was seven years old. Seven was a little younger than eight, which might be good for Jackie, but it wasn't too much younger. Shirley had been hoping Erin could come over, too, since she was Shirley's age and a lot of fun. But Erin was busy.

However, Sessie was already playing with a friend, Joan Novak, and both Sessie and Joan were on their way over.

"You guys could have a tea party," Shirley told Jackie. "Or you could play dress-ups in Mom's old clothes. Or maybe Mom will help you bake cookies or something."

"Dress-ups?" said Jackie. "Prease exprain to me 'dress-ups.'"

Shirley raised her eyebrows. There was so much Jackie didn't know.

As it turned out, she didn't have to explain "dress-ups." Sessie and Joan came over, each carrying a trunk full of Barbie dolls and clothes. They'd been playing Barbie over at the Bayards' house, and they simply moved their game into Shirley and Jackie's bedroom.

Sessie opened her trunk, dumped it out, and began to arrange things. Joan did the same.

"See?" said Sessie. "This is Barbie's ballroom."

"Ballroom?" repeated Shirley. Her eyes glazed over. She hated dolls.

But Jackie looked fascinated. She'd been sitting on her bed; now she moved to the floor. "And what is this?" she asked Joan, peering at her trunk.

"Barbie's movie theater," replied Joan.

"Oh," said Jackie. "See *Rady and Tramp*. (*Lady and the Tramp* was the only movie Jackie had seen.)

"Huh?" said Joan, but she didn't look up from what she was doing.

Jackie moved in to examine the Barbies and their clothes. She spotted a long, filmy, sequined evening gown. "Ooh, pretty!" she cried, touching it.

"Isn't it beautiful?" asked Sessie. "It's new. And Malibu Barbie is going to wear it to the dance tonight. Here, why don't you dress her?" Sessie handed the Barbie and the dress to Jackie, whose eyes were shining.

"Now the other Barbies have to get ready for the dance," added Joan. She began pulling evening gowns and high heels out of the mess of clothes.

"Barbie ready," Jackie announced a few moments later.

"Perfect," said Sessie.

"Now go to dance room!" Jackie cried.

"Right!" said Joan and Sessie.

The three girls walked their dressy Barbies over to Sessie's trunk.

"And the dance begins!" exclaimed Joan.

Shirley left the room. How boring, she thought.

Jackie didn't even notice that Shirley had left.

Shirley walked slowly downstairs. She turned on the TV set and watched cartoons for an hour. Then she went back to her bedroom and stood in the doorway.

Jackie, Sessie, and Joan were still on the floor with the dolls. Jackie was saying, "And then, after zoo, they go to circus!"

And Joan replied, "Yeah, and Barbie rides a wild horse—bareback!"

Shirley tiptoed away. She found her mother in the den, writing letters. "Hey, Mom," she said glumly, "I know what to get Jackie for Christmas."

"What?" replied Mrs. Basini absently.

"Barbie stuff."

Shirley didn't know why she suddenly felt so glum about Jackie and her friends. After all, she had wanted friends for Jackie. Maybe she just hadn't expected Jackie to get along with the girls so quickly. Maybe she'd thought Jackie would need her a little more—like she'd needed her on her first night at the Basinis', and during her first weeks in school.

But Jackie didn't seem to need Shirley at all just then.

That was Saturday. On Monday, Shirley forgot all about feeling hurt. Monday was a great day, a red-letter day. It started when Shirley dropped Jackie off at her first-grade classroom. Jackie walked confidently inside. While she was taking off her coat and boots in front of her cubby, her teacher said to Shirley, "You ought to be proud of Jackie and proud of yourself."

"Why should I be proud of me?" asked Shirley.

"Because," said the teacher, "Jackie is making wonderful progress. Remarkable progress, actually. And you've been a big help to her. Do you know that she's reading as well as the other children in the class? And they've been speaking and hearing English all their lives. Your mother told me about the flash cards you made, and the list of Jackie's words you keep in your room. That's really terrific. Jackie is a very smart girl, but she wouldn't be doing so well without you."

Shirley smiled. Then she grinned. She wished her parents and Joe and Mr. Bradley could hear Jackie's teacher.

"Bye, Jackie!" Shirley called. "I gotta go now. I'll pick you up this afternoon."

"Bye, Shirrey!" Jackie called back.

Shirley also wished Jackie could pronounce her *l*'s. Jackie spoke with an accent. Oh, well. Shirley decided the accent would go away in time. She strode down the hall and into Mr. Bradley's room.

"Good morning, Shirley," said Mr. Bradley pleasantly from behind his desk. "May I see you for a moment?"

Uh-oh. Now what? What test had Shirley failed? What stupid mistake had she made?

Shirley smiled. "Can't you see me from over there?" she asked sweetly.

"I *meant*, I'd like to ask you a question. In private,"

said Mr. Bradley. He sounded somewhat less pleasant.

Shirley put her notebook on her desk, and crossed the room to Mr. Bradley. "Yes?" she said. She bit her lip. She just knew this meant trouble.

Mr. Bradley pointed to Shirley's prizewinning Halloween poster that was still hanging on a wall of the classroom. "You did a great job with the poster," he told her. Shirley nodded. "So I was wondering if you'd like to design a Thanksgiving bulletin board for the class."

"Design a bulletin board? Oh, I don't— I mean, I couldn't—" Shirley stammered.

"You could work on it during recess if you like, or you could stay after school any day I'm here. If you need it, I could probably give you a little class time. What I'd like you to do is come up with an idea that really shows the spirit of Thanksgiving—just like you did with Halloween.

"You can work on it by yourself," Mr. Bradley continued, "or you can ask a few students to help you. But if you do, I want you in charge. By the way, I'll give you extra credit for this."

Shirley's mouth opened wide. She was sure it had opened so wide her chin was resting on the floor. She made an effort to close it.

"What do you say?" asked Mr. Bradley.

"I say yes!" Shirley exclaimed. She could hardly

believe what was happening. Mr. Bradley liked her work. He trusted her. . . . He was going to give her extra credit.

"Great," said Mr. Bradley. "Let me know what materials you need, and if you want anyone to help you."

"Okay," agreed Shirley. "I think I want to work alone, though."

Shirley walked slowly back to her desk. Should she show the first Thanksgiving? Should she show Thanksgiving today? She tried to think how she would explain Thanksgiving to Jackie. Maybe that would help her decide what to do.

Shirley was deep in thought—but when the bell rang, she sat up straight and paid attention to Mr. Bradley. After all, both he and Jackie's teacher seemed to think she was responsible and helpful, and Shirley wanted to prove that they were right.

During social studies that morning, Shirley noticed that Ned Hernandez's underwear was showing. But she didn't jump up and shout, "I see London, I see France, I see Ned's underpants!" She didn't even pass a note about it to anyone. Getting laughs was nice, but getting praise from teachers seemed better just then. And jumping up and shouting was not going to earn Shirley any praise.

When Mr. Bradley made the mistake of saying, "I'm now going to pass out..." Shirley kept her mouth shut—even though she knew her classmates were looking at her, waiting for her to call for the nurse and smelling salts.

During math class, Shirley stared hard at the special work sheet Mr. Bradley set before her. The first problem read: *Two dinosaurs meet on the street. Each one has four feet, and each foot has five toes. How many dinosaur toes are there altogether?*

Shirley started to write "Plenty," but she changed her mind. Instead she drew a picture of two dinosaurs with four feet each and five toes on each foot. Then she counted the toes. Forty! That really was plenty, but all she wrote in the answer blank was 40.

Shirley finished the rest of the work sheet. She didn't raise her hand for help, or call out, "Lunchtime!" when the bell rang, even though she knew Ned Hernandez expected her to. And she thought she'd gotten most of the answers right—maybe all of them.

After recess, Mr. Bradley asked to see her again. Shirley walked over to his desk.

Mr. Bradley didn't say a word. He just held up her math paper. A gold star and a big red 90 were on the top. "Only one wrong, Shirley!" said Mr. Bradley. "I'm really proud of you. This is fantastic!"

Shirley practically fainted. "Could I take this home with me and show it to my parents tonight?" she asked. "Otherwise, they'll never believe it."

"Of course," replied Mr. Bradley.

* * *

Shirley waited until after dinner before she showed the paper to her parents. The dishes had been cleared away, and Mr. and Mrs. Basini were in the living room. Mr. Basini was grading papers. Mrs. Basini was reading *Make Way for Ducklings* to Jackie.

Shirley entered the room.

"Ahem," she said.

Everyone looked at her.

Shirley held up her math sheet. "Ta-*dah*!" she cried. "Ninety percent! Only one wrong."

"Good for you," said Mrs. Basini. "I knew you could do it."

"So did I, peanut!" said Shirley's father. "That is fabulous!" He smiled at Shirley and she smiled back.

"That's not all," Shirley went on. She told her family about the Thanksgiving bulletin board and the extra credit.

"What is Thanksgiving?" asked Jackie.

Shirley and her parents were trying to explain when the phone rang.

"I'll get it!" cried Shirley. She flew into the kitchen. "Hello, Basinis'," she said. "Joe? *Joe!* Hi! How are you?" Shirley leaned around the corner and yelled, "Hey, Mom and Dad, it's Joe!" She stepped back into the kitchen. "When are you coming home?" she asked him. Without waiting for an answer, she told him about the math paper, the bulletin board, and the progress Jackie was making.

"That's super, kiddo. Really super," said Joe. "I can't wait to see the paper—and you, of course."

"And Jackie," Shirley reminded him.

"And Jackie."

"When will you be home?"

"In one week."

"All *right*!"

Shirley had so much to look forward to: her bulletin board, Joe, and all the things she still needed to teach Jackie.

CHAPTER FOUR: *December*

"What do you say we take a vote?" asked Mr. Bradley.

"Yes! Yes!" cried Shirley's classmates.

It was December second. Shirley's Thanksgiving bulletin board was about to come down, but no one wanted to see it go.

Shirley gazed at her work of art. It was good and she knew it. She had decided to show two things in her display—how people get the food for the big meal, from harvesting it in the fields, to serving it at dinner; and how Thanksgiving has changed from the very first holiday to today. So the left side of her bulletin board showed the Indians and the Pilgrims planting seeds, the middle part showed farmers harvesting the fields and then trucks carrying the food to stores, and the right side of the bulletin board showed a modern family (which looked very much like Shirley, her parents, Joe, and Jackie) sitting down to their meal.

Shirley had worked hard on the project. She had cut the figures out of construction paper and glued them together. She had made clouds out of cotton balls, and dirt out of coffee grounds. She had even pulled a desk up to the bulletin board and arranged a cornucopia on it, so that it looked as if the fruits and vegetables were spilling right out of her picture.

Her classmates loved it, she had finished it on time, and Mr. Bradley had given her a big fat A + .

But now it was December and Thanksgiving was over. When the students had come to school that morning and found Mr. Bradley starting to peel the figures off the board, they had protested. Finally Ned Hernandez had said, "I have an idea. Let's name Shirley our Class Artist. She can make a new bulletin board every month."

And that was when Mr. Bradley had said, "What do you say we take a vote?"

As soon as everyone arrived, they did just that.

The vote was unanimous.

Shirley Basini was named Class Artist for Mr. Bradley's room.

I better get thinking, Shirley told herself that morning. I better get right to work on the December bulletin board. I'll do Christmas and Hanukkah, maybe. Or I could do something about winter. Winter starts this month.

Shirley took her responsibilities seriously. Class Artist. What an honor! She couldn't wait to tell her parents. They had been overjoyed about the A+ on the Thanksgiving bulletin board. They had even come to school one afternoon to see it. They had admired the Pilgrims and Indians and cotton balls and coffee grounds before they had gone to Jackie's room for a conference with her teacher.

That wasn't the only good news. Shirley had gotten another 90 on a math paper. And she was almost halfway through her second-grade reading book. With any luck, she'd be using a third-grade reader by the time fourth grade was over. Maybe there was hope for her yet. Maybe she wouldn't have to stay back after all.

Shirley wasn't the only Basini who was doing well that December. Jackie was now the best reader in her class. Her English wasn't bad either. She and Shirley often had long talks at night after their light had been turned off.

"Shirrey," Jackie began one evening from under the warmth of her quilt, "exprain, prease, about Christmas again."

Shirley knew that Jackie just wanted to hear a story, so she decided to tell her about Mary and Joseph and Jesus. "A long, long, *long* time ago," she said, "there lived a mean ruler."

"King Midas?" asked Jackie.

"No," Shirley replied, "he was another ruler. And he wasn't mean, just greedy."

"Exprain 'greedy,' prease," said Jackie.

"Do you really want me to exprain—I mean, explain—or do you want to hear the story?"

"I want the story, prease," answered Jackie.

"All right." Shirley began again. "A long time ago lived a mean ruler named Caesar Augustus, and he decided that he wanted to count all the people he had conquered. You know, to get the population. So he told everyone to go back to their hometowns," Shirley rushed on, before Jackie could say, "Exprain 'popuration,' prease." Shirley paused, thinking. The Christmas story was actually sort of complicated. "This one couple, Mary and Joseph, had a long trip to make to their hometown," she continued, "and when they got there, they couldn't find any place to stay."

"No empty rooms in the motor rodge?" Jackie spoke up.

"Inn," Shirley corrected her.

"In what?"

Shirley sighed. "Finally, Mary and Joseph asked this innkeeper if they could just sleep in his stable—his barn—that night. It was really important because Mary was going to have a baby."

"She was pregnant," Jackie said proudly.

"Uh, right." Shirley told Jackie about the angel Gabriel, the birth of Jesus, the shepherds, and the three wise men. "And that," she said at last, "is why we celebrate Christmas. Isn't that a great story?"

Shirley heard only silence.

"Jackie?" she said. "Jackie?"

Jackie murmured something and rolled over.

"I don't believe it," said Shirley, peering across the room at her sister. "Sound asleep."

But when Shirley woke up the next morning, Jackie was already up. She was leaning against her pillow, her bedside light on, reading a book called *Leo and Emily*. *Leo and Emily* wasn't exactly a long chapter book like Mrs. Basini was always urging Shirley to read, but it was no picture book either.

Jackie looked up and saw her sister. "Good morning," she said with a grin.

"Morning," mumbled Shirley. "What are you doing?"

"Reading," replied Jackie, in a tone that meant it should be obvious.

"I *know*, but how come you're reading *now*? It's so early."

"Not earry. Good time to read. I rike Reo and Emiry."

"Leo and Emily," Shirley corrected her crossly. She wasn't sure why she felt so grumpy, but she knew it had something to do with Jackie's reading. Jackie was becoming a bookworm and Mrs. Basini loved it.

"Do you know all the words in that book?" asked Shirley.

"I can *read* them aw," Jackie answered thoughtfully. "If I don't understand, I rook up!" She pulled a children's dictionary out from under her bed.

"Where'd you get that?" Shirley wanted to know.

"Mommy buy it for me . . . *bought* it for me."

"Hmphh," hmphhed Shirley. When had her mother done that? And why did Jackie insist on calling their mother "Mommy"? It was so babyish. Shirley had been calling her "Mom" for years. Practically since she started talking.

"You know how to use that thing?" asked Shirley.

"Dictionary?" replied Jackie. "Sure. See? Right now, I rook up 'apprauded.' Very rong word. And I need to rook up 'hocus-pocus.'"

"Good luck finding it," said Shirley. She rolled out of bed and began to get dressed. "You better get dressed now, too," she added. "You don't want to be late."

At breakfast that morning, Mrs. Basini said, "I'm working at the library this afternoon, girls. Shirley, would you walk Jackie over after school, please?"

"Why?" replied Shirley who was in only a slightly better mood. "What's going on? Another story hour?" This wasn't the first time Mrs. Basini had asked Shirley to bring Jackie to the children's room at the public library on one of the days she was working there. She had asked her to do it every time there was to be a special event. According to Mrs. Basini, special events involving reading were helpful to Jackie, her English, and her schoolwork.

"No, not story hour," replied Shirley's mother. "Jackie just wants to take out a few more books, don't you, honey?"

"A stack!" exclaimed Jackie, looking the way most people do when they think about chocolate cake or birthdays. "More Reo and Emiry. Maybe a Betsy and Eddie book. Want to read Ritter Bear books again, too."

"*Ritter* Bear?" repeated Shirley.

Mrs. Basini looked up sharply. "She means Little Bear, Shirley. Give her a chance."

Her father added gently, "This is important for Jackie, honey."

But Shirley felt wounded. She put down her glass of orange juice. "Maybe I can't bring her today," she said. "Maybe I'm busy."

Now Jackie looked wounded. She glanced from Shirley to Mr. and Mrs. Basini. "I can come myseff," she said quietly. "I know way. Never mind, Shirrey. Don't worry."

"I wasn't worried," said Shirley coldly, but she felt bad anyway. Not bad enough, however, to say that she would walk Jackie to the library after all.

So that afternoon Jackie walked herself there. Since she had proved that she could walk there alone, she began walking to the library and taking out a pile of books every single time Mrs. Basini was working.

Shirley tried to feel grouchy about this, but it was hard. Christmas was coming! She was working on a new bulletin board, she had all sorts of holiday things to teach Jackie, and Joe would be home again soon. One afternoon (while Jackie was at the library with Mrs. Basini), Mr. Bradley stayed after school to work on his lesson plans, so Shirley stayed, too.

"Mr. Bradley," she told him, "I decided something about the December bulletin board."

"What's that, Shirley?"

"I'm not going to make a bulletin board about a holiday. If I make a Christmas scene, then I leave the Jewish kids out. If I make a Hanukkah scene, then I leave the Christian kids out. I was going to try to do both, but it's too hard. So I'm going to do something with toys. Toys are kind of for Christmas and Hanukkah both, don't you think?"

"Well—" began Mr. Bradley.

"I mean, you get presents in December whether you're Christian or Jewish, right? And if you're a kid, a lot of those presents are toys, right? So my bulletin board is going to show an enchanted toy store—with the toys coming to life."

"That sounds wonderful, Shirley," said Mr. Bradley. "Very imaginative."

Shirley got out the construction paper, the scissors, and a pencil, and began drawing and snipping away.

Her bulletin board was coming along so well that by the time she got home that day she was in a great mood. She didn't even mind the sight of Jackie sitting cross-legged on her bed surrounded by books.

"How is burretin board?" asked Jackie when she saw Shirley.

"Terrific!" Shirley exclaimed. She told Jackie about the toys. "I wanted to make Santa's workshop, but that's Christmas, so I decided on a toy store instead."

"Exprain 'Santa's workshop,' prease," said Jackie.

"You know, the workshop where Santa Claus and his elves make the toys."

"Santa Craus?"

"Whoa," said Shirley under her breath. She whistled softly. "You don't know about Santa Claus, do you?"

"No," replied Jackie, looking down at her books as if they could help. "Exprain, prease."

Shirley did better than that. She talked to her parents, and the next Saturday, the four Basinis drove to Grove Mall. It was snowing lightly, and Shirley thought she could almost *smell* Christmas. It was all around her.

"You're going to love this holiday," she told Jackie. "It's more than the Christmas story I told you. It's snow and cookies and a decorated tree."

"It's Santa Claus and toys and a stuffed stocking," added Mrs. Basini.

"Christmas carols and eggnog and a nice, warm fire," added Mr. Basini.

"And ten days off from school," said Shirley.

The Basinis had been explaining Christmas endlessly to Jackie. And that day, Jackie was going to see her first Santa Claus, at the department store in the mall.

The mall, Shirley thought, was really something. It glittered and shone with decorations. A group of carolers strolled from store to store singing Christmas songs. A man dressed like an elf was handing out candy canes. But most exciting, on the eighth floor of the department store was Santa's World.

The Basinis stepped off the escalator and walked through a doorway made of giant Styrofoam candy canes. Ahead of them was a big gingerbready-looking house, decorated with candy and snow.

Jackie's eyes were shining. "The North Poe," she said, reading a sign. "This way to Santa Craus."

A line of children and their parents had formed outside the gingerbread house. Most of the kids were a lot younger than Shirley and Jackie, but Shirley didn't mind. She couldn't wait to see Jackie's face when she sat in Santa's lap. Jackie had been reading *The Night Before Christmas*, and was more excited than

Shirley had ever seen her. Mr. Basini planned to take her picture while she was talking to Santa Claus.

The line crept along. Jackie began wriggling with excitement. When at last it was her turn to step into Santa's castle, she whispered. "Hode my hand, prease, Shirrey."

So Shirley stayed with Jackie who sat down in Santa's lap, looking awed.

"And what do you want for Christmas, little lady?" asked the jolly Santa Claus.

"I want—I want," whispered Jackie, "to go to school. And to be friend of Sessie and Joan. And to stay with Basinis. And to be Shirrey's sister forever."

"Don't you want any toys?" asked the Santa, looking slightly surprised.

"Could I have a book?" asked Jackie.

"Certainly! Ho, ho, ho! Which book?"

"Any book," Jackie whispered. Then she added, "Thank you," and managed a smile before she slid off Santa's lap.

Flash! went Mr. Basini's camera.

And that was Jackie Basini's meeting with Santa Claus.

On the last day of school before vacation, Mr. and Mrs. Basini came to Shirley's classroom. They arrived at two-thirty, just as Mr. Bradley was saying goodbye to his students.

Shirley proudly showed off the December bulletin board. Her parents were very impressed.

"Lovely," said Mrs. Basini.

"Magnificent," said Mr. Basini.

"We can't wait to see what she'll do for January," added Mr. Bradley.

Then Shirley's parents rushed off. Jackie's teacher had asked them to come in for a conference. Shirley wondered what Jackie had done wrong. Teachers only asked for conferences when there were problems. She and Jackie waited on the front steps of the school while the adults talked.

"Were you late for anything?" asked Shirley.

Jackie shook her head.

"Did you hit anybody?"

Jackie shook her head. "No. I don't hurt anybody. I am never rate. I best reader. I best in math. I finish with math book and work in another. I do nothing bad."

"Okay, okay," said Shirley.

When Mr. and Mrs. Basini finally came outside, they were grinning from ear to ear.

"*Won*derful news!" exclaimed Mrs. Basini. "Guess what, Jackie?"

"What?" replied Jackie. "I do nothing bad."

"No, of course not, sweetheart. You did something very *good*. You worked so hard that after vacation, you are going to go to third grade!"

"Third!" cried Shirley. "What happened to second? And the rest of first?"

"She's skipping them," said Mr. Basini. He put his arm around Shirley. Shirley knew that he understood how she felt—stupid and left behind.

"Not only that," went on Mrs. Basini, "but Jackie is going to enter *Mrs. Rockwell*'s third grade."

Shirley nearly fainted. Mrs. Rockwell's class was the special, excelled one for very, very smart third graders. There was one special class like hers in every grade. Shirley had never been in one (but Joe had). She couldn't believe it. Jackie would practically be doing fourth-grade work, while some of Shirley's work was still for second graders.

Mr. and Mrs. Basini were hugging Jackie and telling her how proud they were. Shirley turned away. Her parents were hardly ever proud of her. Except maybe for things like her bulletin boards. But bulletin boards were not the same as being moved to Mrs. Rockwell's class. Shirley had worked hard all fall, and look where it had gotten her. Nowhere.

Shirley could have killed Jackie. This just wasn't fair. It really wasn't. Having a sister as smart as Jackie was worse than having a brother as smart as Joe.

Christmas was ruined.

Everything was ruined.

Shirley decided she hated Jackie.

CHAPTER FIVE: *January*

January was dreary. It was dark and wet and gloomy. The holidays were over. Vacation was over. School had started again. The only one who seemed happy about it was Jackie. She loved Mrs. Rockwell. She loved the library in her new third-grade classroom. For Jackie, January was just more time to read.

For Shirley, January was the beginning of the end. Well, she wasn't sure about that, but she thought there was a good chance of it. Besides, she liked the way that sounded.

Shirley's January bulletin board was as dreary as everything else. There were no important holidays in January except New Year's Day, and Shirley had never thought much of that holiday. So, the Class Artist decided that her bulletin board would be about winter. She created a farm in late afternoon with a snowstorm brewing. Great black clouds were rolling in, and the snow that had already fallen was whirling and swirling and blowing around the house and barn and dark fir trees. The effect was frightening. Everyone in Mr. Bradley's class agreed that it was a very good bulletin board—but that they couldn't wait for the nice red-and-white one they were certain the Class Artist would make for February.

One Monday late in January, sleet began to fall. It began to fall during math, which was in the middle of the morning. The sky grew darker and darker until it was as dark as Shirley's threatening clouds on the bulletin board.

Nobody could concentrate on their math problems. Shirley and her classmates gazed out the windows at the wet, black schoolyard.

"Oh," groaned Ned, "no recess today. We'll have to stay inside."

"Maybe it will stop," said Shirley, but she didn't really think it would.

And as if to prove a point, the sleet suddenly began to fall harder, lashing noisily against the windows.

Mr. Bradley looked sympathetically at his students. "It could be worse," he said.

"How?" asked Shirley.

Mr. Bradley thought for a moment. "It would be

worse if you didn't have a wonderful teacher like me who would let you spend your recess in here playing seven-up and hot and cold and who's got the button?"

Nobody said a word, and Shirley knew why. That wasn't so special. It was what Mr. Bradley suggested every time they couldn't use the playground.

Just then, the door to the classroom opened, and in came Mrs. Rockwell. She was followed by her students. Jackie was the third one to enter the room, and she smiled shyly at Shirley.

When the entire class was assembled at the front of Mr. Bradley's room, Mrs. Rockwell said, "Today is gloomy and dreary. Everyone is in a bad mood. And so—"

(Mrs. Rockwell looked at Mr. Bradley, and Shirley got the feeling that this whole thing—whatever it was—had been planned.)

"Yes?" said Mr. Bradley.

Mrs. Rockwell's students spoke as one. "Our class challenges your class to a spelling bee this afternoon."

"Do you accept?" Mrs. Rockwell asked Mr. Bradley.

"Do you accept?" Mr. Bradley asked Shirley and her classmates.

"Yes!" shouted his students—except for one.

That one was Shirley.

Shirley was a terrible speller, and now she would have to compete against her own little sister.

Jackie, of course, was a wonderful speller. She might not have been a wonderful speaker, since she was still learning new words and sometimes mixed them up or didn't pronounce them right. But she was a wonderful speller. Just like she was a wonderful reader, a wonderful adder, a wonderful subtracter, and a wonderful memorizer.

"She's like a sponge," Mrs. Basini had said over the Christmas holiday. "She's a very smart girl. Her mind just soaks up information and then wrings it out again in other forms."

That was something Mrs. Basini had never said about Shirley. Shirley knew she wouldn't be happy until her mother called her a sponge, too.

Shirley tried to figure out what to do about the spelling bee. How could she get out of it? Only once had she gone to the nurse when she wasn't actually sick or hurt. The nurse had sent her home, but Mrs. Basini had figured out what Shirley was up to. She'd been very cross. Going to the nurse wouldn't work.

Shirley raised her hand.

"Yes, Shirley?" said Mr. Bradley. The third graders were gone. The students of 4C were bent over their math books again.

"Um, I can't be in the spelling bee this afternoon," Shirley began.

"Oh, really?" Mr. Bradley replied.

"No. I have to work on the bulletin board."

"Isn't it finished?" Mr. Bradley glanced at the dark farmhouse.

"Yes, it is. It's just that I think I better change it before Mrs. Rockwell's kids come back. They're only eight years old. I'm afraid the bulletin board will scare them."

"I think they can handle it," said Mr. Bradley dryly.

That was the end of that. Shirley was out of ideas. If only Mrs. Rockwell had given a little more warning.

At one-thirty that afternoon, right after the games of seven-up and hot and cold and who's got the button? were over, Mrs. Rockwell and her class returned. The third graders lined up along one side of the classroom. "Now, my people," said Mr. Bradley (Shirley hated being called a "people"), "please line up on the other side of the room."

With a great rush and a clatter, the fourth graders formed a line. They leaned against the blackboard and grinned at the third graders.

Shirley made sure she was next to Ned Hernandez. She had a last-ditch plan for getting through the spelling bee (or maybe getting out of it). Ned might come in handy.

Shirley also made sure that she and Ned were close

to the back of the room, which meant they were near the end of the line—and across from Jackie.

"Students," said Mrs. Rockwell, clapping her hands, "let me explain the rules of the spelling bee. Mr. Bradley will say the words that you are to spell. He'll say each word only once. You are to repeat the word, spell it, and repeat it again. If you spell it correctly, move to the end of the line. If you misspell it, take a seat. The winning team will be the one with the most players left when the bell rings at the end of the day. Are there any questions?"

Shirley waved her hand wildly. "What's the prize?" she asked.

"Excuse me?" said Mrs. Rockwell.

Shirley adjusted her glasses. "What do the winners get?"

Mrs. Rockwell glanced at Mr. Bradley who said lightly, "No prizes, Shirley. We're just playing for fun."

Some fun, thought Shirley.

Then she raised her hand again. "Can you please say the rules once more?" she asked Mrs. Rockwell.

Mrs. Rockwell patiently repeated the rules.

"Thank you," said Shirley.

"All right," began Mrs. Rockwell.

Crash.

All eyes turned toward the back of the room where Shirley had knocked over a big tin full of crayons.

Ned stooped down to help her pick them up. At the same time, Shirley heard a voice say, "I hepp Shirrey, prease?"

"Thank you, Jackie," Mrs. Rockwell replied, "but Shirley and her friend can pick them up themselves. And," she added sternly, looking at Shirley, "we're going to start the spelling bee now anyway."

Darn, thought Shirley as she and Ned tossed crayons back into the tin. Mrs. Rockwell was tough. She wouldn't delay the spelling bee no matter what. How come Jackie liked her so much?

The contest began. Mr. Bradley gave the first word to the first third grader. "Machine," he said clearly.

"Machine," the girl repeated. "M-A-C-H-I-N-E. Machine."

"Very good," said Mr. Bradley. "Go to the end of your line." He turned to Jason Rice in Shirley's class. "Sign," he said.

Shirley stopped listening. The crayons had been put away. She picked up a piece of chalk and began to draw a monster on the blackboard behind her. She added a bubble by the monster's mouth and printed the word ʙᴜʀᴘ inside. She hoped it was spelled right.

It must have been, because Ned and a bunch of other kids began giggling.

"Shirley," warned Mr. Bradley, "erase that, please."

Shirley erased the monster.

Jason moved to the end of the line and Mr. Bradley gave out the next spelling word. The game continued. The lines moved forward as kids either dropped out or walked to the back of the room.

Shirley made a pig nose at Ned. She made pig noses at several of the third graders.

"Young lady," said Mrs. Rockwell to Shirley, just before it was Jackie's turn, "one more stunt and you'll be out of the spelling bee."

"No, she won't," Mr. Bradley jumped in. "No matter how many stunts Shirley pulls, she'll take part in the game. But keep in mind, Shirley, that the principal's office is just around the corner."

Shirley had been preparing to belch while Jackie spelled her word. *Darn*, she thought again. She tried to let the saved-up air out of her chest quietly.

"All right, Jackie," said Mr. Bradley, "are you ready?"

Jackie nodded. She glanced nervously at Shirley, but Shirley didn't feel like smiling at her.

"Present," said Mr. Bradley.

"Present," repeated Jackie. "P-R-E-S-E-N-T. Present."

"Good! Move to the back of your line."

Jackie, smiling, moved to the end of the third-grade line, where Mrs. Rockwell gave her a hug.

Shirley rolled her eyes in disgust. But she was too

close to the head of her line to think much about Jackie.

It was Ned's turn and he misspelled "prize." He sat down at his desk and began reading a comic book.

When it was Shirley's turn, Mr. Bradley gave her the word "trick." Shirley wanted to join Ned. But she didn't want to look as if she weren't as smart as Jackie. She took a deep breath and said, "Trick. T-R-I-C-K. Trick."

"Very good," Mr. Bradley told her.

"Hurray, Shirrey!" cried Jackie.

Shirley ignored her. She walked to the back of the fourth-grade line.

The game went on and on. When Jackie was up next, Mr. Bradley gave her the word "telephone."

"Terephone," Jackie repeated.

A few kids snickered, but Jackie spelled the word right. Shirley thought her sister looked a bit smug as she returned to the end of the line.

Mr. Bradley turned to Shirley. "Elephant," he said.

Elephant! What a long word. Shirley had no idea how to spell it. But she knew how to get a laugh. And if she was going to be out of the game, she wanted a laugh, at least. "Erephant," said Shirley. "E-R-E-"

The kids exploded into laughter—except for Jackie, whose eyes filled with tears.

"Shirley!" Mr. Bradley admonished her. "Take your seat this minute."

Shirley picked up her chair and carried it out of the classroom.

"That does it," said Mr. Bradley. "You can carry that to the principal's office. I'll come with you. Mrs. Rockwell, will you take over here, please?"

"Of course," replied Mrs. Rockwell.

Mr. Bradley followed Shirley and her chair right into the principal's office. He didn't say a word except to the office secretary. "I'd like to speak with Mrs. Hillier," he said briefly.

The secretary nodded.

Then Mr. Bradley took the chair from Shirley and banged it onto the floor. He pointed to it, indicating that Shirley should sit on it.

Shirley sat, feeling horrible. She had never seen Mr. Bradley so cross.

Shirley Basini would just as soon forget what happened during the rest of the day. First, Mr. Bradley went into Mrs. Hillier's office for a while. When he came out, he returned to the classroom. He still had not spoken to Shirley. Then Mrs. Hillier called Shirley into her office.

Shirley sat in a chair next to Mrs. Hillier's desk. She waited while the principal closed the door to the office. Mrs. Hillier talked to Shirley for a long time. Mr. Bradley was mad that Shirley had misbehaved during the spelling bee, but he was mostly mad about what she had done to Jackie.

Shirley began to worry. Was Mr. Bradley mad enough to make her repeat fourth grade after all? No. Embarrassing Jackie couldn't cause that...could it? If it could, Shirley and Jackie would be in the same grade the next year, only Jackie would probably be in the special class for smart kids. Shirley couldn't stand it.

The last thing that happened was that Mrs. Hillier called Mrs. Basini to tell her about Shirley's behavior.

That night, Shirley got the talking-to of her life. Her parents waited until dinner was over. While Jackie was doing her homework, they took Shirley into the den, sat her on the couch, and stood in front of her.

"We're very disappointed in you," said her mother. "Being rude and disruptive is bad enough. Being sent to Mrs. Hillier is bad enough."

"But teasing Jackie that way," her father continued, "is not acceptable. I know that competing against Jackie in the spelling bee must have been difficult for you. But you embarrassed her in front of all of her new classmates."

Shirley slouched down on the couch. She didn't know what to say. Jackie had avoided her all afternoon. At dinner, she wouldn't talk to Shirley, and she kept looking away from her with wounded eyes.

"Getting a new sister was tough," Mr. Basini went

on thoughtfully. "And you were nervous about the spelling bee today. So in order to take the attention away from yourself, you made fun of Jackie. But you hurt her in the worst possible way. That's called finding a person's Achilles' heel, and it's not a nice thing to do."

"Maybe you didn't mean to hurt Jackie as much as you did," added her mother, "but it happened anyway—and we don't want it to happen again. We're going to ground you for two days, starting tomorrow."

Shirley nodded numbly. She'd been in trouble before, but she'd never been grounded.

"Think of Jackie," were her parents' last words that night. "Think of what she's been through, and of how hard she's tried since she moved here."

Over the next few days, Shirley did think about it. She had plenty of time to do so. This was partly because she was grounded, and partly because Jackie was so upset that she temporarily moved into Joe's bedroom. She didn't even want to be *near* Shirley.

But Shirley also kept thinking, What about *me*? I try hard, too. School hasn't been a picnic. But no one cares about anyone except Jackie.

Shirley breathed a sigh of relief when January ended and another month began. She needed a new beginning.

CHAPTER SIX: *February*

After the spelling bee, Shirley was afraid that Mr. Bradley might take away her Class Artist title. But he didn't. He never mentioned it. He didn't mention the spelling bee either. In fact, the day after the spelling bee—the first day that Shirley was grounded—Mr. Bradley seemed to be regular old Mr. Bradley again.

February arrived with a whirl of snow and one gray day after another. Shirley didn't feel any more cheerful than she had in January, but she decided to make a nice, bright red-and-white bulletin board anyway. She knew her classmates wanted one. So she set to work on an imaginary place called "The Heart Factory." It showed funny little gnomes and elves spinning wheels and pulling levers to make hearts for people to send on Valentine's Day. She found that working on the bulletin board made her feel better.

It even made her feel better on the day Mr. Bradley called her to his desk just before lunchtime.

"Yes?" said Shirley nervously. She watched her classmates hustle out the door and down the hall to the cafeteria.

"Shirley," Mr. Bradley began. He looked serious, but not cross. "Shirley," he said again, "at the beginning of the school year your work was far below par. It wasn't up to fourth-grade standards."

Shirley nodded.

"During the fall you made some improvement. Especially in math. We were working hard together, as we had promised each other, and I was proud of you. But ever since Christmas your work has been slipping. I don't want to see you stay back next year."

"I don't want to see me stay back either."

"Good. I'm glad to hear that," Mr. Bradley told Shirley. "Are you willing to try something that might help you pull your work up?"

"I guess..." said Shirley slowly. It depended on what the something was.

"All right. Starting today, I'd like you to spend one hour every afternoon working with Mr. Soderman in the Resource Room. I think you'll like him," Mr. Bradley added.

"Is this my last chance or something?" asked Shirley. She still didn't want to be in a class with a bunch of retards, but she was willing to give it a shot.

"No, but I strongly suggest that you try it," said Mr. Bradley.

"Is Mr. Soderman going to give me extra homework?"

"I don't think so. Don't worry about it." Mr. Bradley smiled slyly.

Shirley worked with Mr. Soderman that very afternoon. As soon as lunch and recess were over, Mr. Bradley signaled to her that it was time to go to the Resource Room.

Shirley tiptoed to his desk. "What should I take with me?" she whispered. (She didn't want the kids to know where she was going.)

"Nothing," Mr. Bradley replied. "Just yourself."

Shirley was mystified. Wasn't Mr. Soderman supposed to help her with her work? How could he do that if she didn't take it along?

Shirley reached the door to the Resource Room. She peeked inside. Two kids she didn't know were working at a table with a woman. A young man was kneeling by a shelf, looking through some books. When Shirley opened the door, he straightened up.

"Shirley Basini?" he asked.

Shirley nodded. She closed the door behind her.

"I'm Mr. Soderman," said the man. "I guess we're going to be working together for a while. Why don't you come over here and take a look at these books."

Shirley crossed the room to the shelf. It looked like a little piece of the children's room at the public library—four rows of books covered with shiny plastic. There were picture books, easy reading books, and chapter books.

Mr. Soderman pulled one of the long chapter books off the shelf. "Ever heard of this?" he asked. "It's called *Henry and Ribsy*."

Shirley shook her head. It looked like the kind of thing her parents were always trying to get her to read. "I don't like books," she said boldly.

"You don't like books, or you don't like to read?" asked Mr. Soderman.

Shirley paused. She hadn't thought about it. "I guess I don't like to read," she replied.

"Well, that's fixable. It would be another thing if you didn't like the books themselves." Mr. Soderman suddenly made a terrible face. He dropped *Henry and Ribsy* on the floor. "Ew! Yuck!" he exclaimed. "A book! Oh, gross. I am going to be sick!"

Shirley giggled.

Mr. Soderman picked the book up. "Not liking to read—that's something I can take care of. Not liking books would be a problem. You'd have to learn how to read with oven mitts on. Now, let's look at your situation a little more closely."

"Okay," said Shirley, still laughing. She was picturing herself reading with big mitts on her hands.

"Do you dislike stories, too?" asked Mr. Soderman. "Or is it just the reading part?"

"It's the reading part. I like stories."

"Good. Then I guarantee that you will like *Henry and Ribsy*. Come over here."

Mr. Soderman led Shirley to a quiet corner of the room. Cushions covered the floor. Mr. Soderman sat on one, leaned against the wall, and put another behind his back. Shirley sat, too. She made herself comfortable.

Mr. Soderman opened the book and began to read aloud. He read to Shirley for the rest of the hour. Shirley listened—and giggled. *Henry and Ribsy* was the funniest story she'd ever heard.

When the hour was over she asked, "Can we read more of *Henry and Ribsy* tomorrow?"

"Sure," replied Mr. Soderman. "And just in case you were wondering, the book is by an author named Beverly Cleary. She's written lots of other books. Some of them are about Henry, too."

"There are more books about Henry?" Shirley exclaimed. She hadn't meant to sound excited, but she couldn't help it. "Are they funny, too?"

"They're pretty funny. Now you better get back to Mr. Bradley," said Mr. Soderman. "I'll see you tomorrow afternoon."

When Shirley went to the Resource Room the next

day, Mr. Soderman did read *Henry and Ribsy* again. A few days after that, they finished it. Then they began a book about a bear named Paddington. When they were finished with that, Mr. Soderman showed Shirley a book called *Tales of a Fourth Grade Nothing*. Shirley liked the title.

"It's another funny book," said her new teacher. "And do you know how we can make it funnier?"

"How?" asked Shirley suspiciously.

"By reading it like a play. You read the part of Fudge."

Shirley didn't think much of having to read, but she couldn't help saying, "Fudge! Who's Fudge?"

"He's Peter Hatcher's little brother. He's a pest. He gets into mischief."

"I like people who get into mischief," said Shirley.

Mr. Soderman opened *Tales of a Fourth Grade Nothing*. He did most of the reading. But every time Fudge was supposed to say something, Shirley read instead. Fudge was very funny. Shirley hardly felt as if she were reading.

By the end of February, Mr. Soderman was reading less and less and Shirley was reading more and more. Mr. Soderman picked out a book for her called *Pippi Longstocking*. He didn't read a word of it. Shirley read the entire thing. Sometimes she read aloud and sometimes she read to herself. One afternoon she sneaked the book home and read it while everyone else was

out. Some of the words, like "preferred" and "inhab-
ited" and "Villa Villekulla," were very hard, but
Shirley finished the book anyway because she wished
she could be just like Pippi.

After a while, she and Mr. Soderman didn't just
read all the time. Once, Mr. Soderman asked Shirley
to write a different ending to the Paddington book.
That was hard since Shirley had liked Mr. Michael
Bond's ending very much. (He was the author.) But
she worked hard and wrote a new ending anyway.
Mr. Soderman thought Shirley's ending was so good
that he made copies of it. He put her original copy on
the bulletin board in the Resource Room with a blue
ribbon attached to it—just as if it had won a prize.
He gave one copy to Mr. Bradley. He gave another
copy to Shirley. He folded the third copy into an envelope and sent it home with Shirley to give to her
parents.

Shirley was amazed. As far as she knew, no one had
ever liked any of Jackie's work enough to copy it.

One day Shirley asked Mr. Soderman, "How come
we don't read any more of the books about Henry?"

"Well," he replied, "for one thing, I want you to
try some different authors—Michael Bond and Judy
Blume and Astrid Lindgren. And for another, I don't
have any of the others here in the Resource Room."

Shirley smiled. She liked teachers who told the
truth. "Well, where are they?" she wanted to know.

"What if I wanted to read another Henry book?"

"You could go to the library," said Mr. Soderman. "Either our school library or the public library."

Shirley decided not to go to the school library. She didn't want Mr. Bradley to see her there. She didn't want a lot of questions or any pressure about reading. Plus, she didn't want Mr. Bradley to know that his Resource Room plan had worked so well that she was getting interested in books. It was better if teachers didn't know too much about you. Shirley would have to go to the public library—on a day when her mother wasn't working. For the same reasons that she didn't want Mr. Bradley to see her in the school library, she didn't want her mother to see her in the public library.

On Mrs. Basini's next day off, Shirley told her she was going to go over to Erin Bayard's house after school. Then, as soon as school let out, she made a beeline for the public library and went straight to the children's room.

She stood there, feeling helpless. She was surrounded by books. Thousands of books. How was she supposed to find the ones about Henry?

"May I help you?" asked a librarian.

Shirley jumped. She looked guiltily at the woman and was relieved to see that she wasn't one of her mother's friends.

"I want to read a book about Henry," Shirley whispered.

"About Henry? Do you know who the author is?"

Shirley racked her brain. "Beverly Clearly," she finally replied.

"Oh, Beverly *Cleary*. Her books are right over here."

The librarian led Shirley to a bookshelf. "All these books are by Beverly Cleary," she told her.

"*All* of them?" Shirley was awed.

"Well, they're not all about Henry. Only some of them are. But you might like the others, too."

"Okay," said Shirley. "Thanks."

The Beverly Cleary books were on the two bottom shelves, so Shirley sat on the floor and began to read the titles. *Beezus and Ramona*. (What's a Beezus? Shirley wondered.) *Dear Mr. Henshaw, Ellen Tebbits, Fifteen*. None of those books sounded as if they were about Henry.

That was just what Shirley was thinking when she came to the next book, *Henry and Beezus*. "Goody," whispered Shirley. Now she could find out what a Beezus was, too. Shirley glanced down the row of books. The next book was about Henry. So was the next one—and the next one and the next one. Then came a bunch of other books, including a couple about a mouse, then a whole lot about that girl named

Ramona. And *then* Shirley found a book that was called simply *Ribsy*.

"Ribsy!" Shirley exclaimed softly, and pulled that book off the shelf and set it on top of *Henry and Beezus*. She hadn't liked Ribsy *quite* as much as she'd liked Henry in *Henry and Ribsy*, but she'd liked him an awful lot.

There were a few more of Beverly Cleary's books at the right end of the bottom shelf, but Shirley didn't look at them. She was too busy deciding between *Henry and Beezus* and *Ribsy*, and wondering where she could read the book she chose. She needed a private place.

But where could she find one? How about Joe's room? Nah. Jackie had long since moved back in with Shirley, but anyone could find Shirley in Joe's bedroom. The attic? Maybe, but there were spiders in the attic. The tree house? That was a good idea. Joe and Mr. Basini had built a really spectacular tree house in the backyard, and Shirley could easily—

"Shirrey! Shirrey! Hi, Shirrey!"

Shirley's stomach flip-flopped. She didn't have to look up to know who was standing over her.

"Hi, Jackie," said Shirley in a small voice, "what are you doing here?"

"Mommy and I came. Mommy remember something she has to do here. She—"

"Shirley! I thought you were playing at Erin's this afternoon," said Mrs. Basini's voice.

Shirley finally looked up. "I was going to," she said, "but Erin had to, um . . ."

"Well, it doesn't matter," Mrs. Basini jumped in. "The point is, you came to the *library* instead." She sounded amazed. And very pleased. But then she said the last thing Shirley would have expected: "Well, I've got a few things to take care of, so I'll meet you girls at the checkout desk in half an hour. How's that?"

"Fine," replied Shirley. So her mother wasn't going to bug her after all. She relaxed.

Jackie dropped onto the floor beside Shirley. "What are these books?" she asked, as Mrs. Basini hurried off.

"They're by Beverly Cleary. . . . Don't you know her?" Shirley had thought Jackie knew everything there was to know about books.

"No," said Jackie. She looked at the two on the floor and read the titles out loud. "Exprain 'Beezus,' prease, Shirrey."

"I don't know what it is either," Shirley told her honestly, "but I'm going to find out." She picked up the books and hugged them to her. "These are mine," she said. "I'm taking them out." Suddenly she wanted both of them. But she felt a little greedy, so she said,

"You should read *this* book. It's really great." She pulled *Henry and Ribsy* off the shelf and handed it to her sister.

"Okay," replied Jackie. "Thank you. You think I am going to rike stories by Beverry Creary?"

"I know so. Oh, and hey! There's another author, Judy Blume, only I don't know where her books are. . . ."

"Brume, Brume," said Jackie. "I think they must be over here." She moved down the stack of books. "Here they are, Shirrey!"

"How did you know that?" asked Shirley.

Jackie explained how the library worked, and Shirley wished she'd paid more attention when Mr. Bradley had talked about alphabetical order. Then Shirley showed *Tales of a Fourth Grade Nothing*, *A Bear Called Paddington*, and *Pippi Longstocking* to Jackie who decided to take out all three, plus *Henry and Ribsy*. Jackie couldn't believe that Shirley had already read them.

After that, Jackie showed *James and the Giant Peach* and *Stuart Little* and *Winnie-the-Pooh* to Shirley. Shirley was interested, but she didn't take them. Two were enough.

That night Shirley and Jackie did their homework together in their bedroom. Lately Shirley had been doing her homework a little more easily. And she got lots more of the answers right. Plus, the more she read the easier reading became.

"Lights out!" Mrs. Basini called at nine-thirty, and Shirley decided it was time to teach Jackie another American custom. She found her flashlight in her top bureau drawer. Then she tiptoed into Joe's room and found *his* flashlight. She gave it to Jackie.

Both girls ducked under their covers and stayed up late reading. Jackie read *Henry and Ribsy,* and Shirley read *Henry and Beezus.*

CHAPTER SEVEN: *March*

By the beginning of March, Shirley had read both *Henry and Beezus* and *Ribsy*. She and Jackie had returned their books to the library. With Jackie's help, Shirley had chosen a new one, *James and the Giant Peach*, and had checked it out. It looked like a very difficult book (even the author's name was hard— Roald Dahl), but Shirley wanted to try it anyway. She liked the idea of traveling around inside a giant peach with giant insects as your only companions, which is just what happens to James, the boy in the story.

She liked the idea so much that she'd decided to put giant insects on her March bulletin board. Since spring began in March, the Class Artist had wanted to create a garden scene. But not just a regular garden scene. Shirley was making a garden the way she imagined one would appear if she could look at it under a microscope.

She had cut out a two-foot-long grasshopper, a fly with eyes the size of pot lids, a ladybug that looked like a spotted basketball, and a butterfly with the wingspan of a crow. She also added a snake so large she could only show its head peeking into the garden, and a gigantic rabbit's paw about to step into the scene. All these animals were playing among flower stalks—big strips of paper that stretched from the top to the bottom of the bulletin board like green pillars. Shirley's classmates were fascinated by her newest project. Every day they looked at it to see how it was coming along.

One windy Tuesday, Shirley asked Mr. Bradley for permission to stay inside during recess. She was almost done with her garden and wanted to work on the final touches. Mr. Bradley gave her permission, even though he was going to be at a meeting.

"No wild parties in the room while I'm not here," was all he said to Shirley.

Shirley had been hard at work for the first ten minutes of recess when she heard the door to the classroom open quietly. Without looking up from the gigantic flower bud she was making, she said, "See, Mr. Bradley? No wild parties. It's just me and the insects."

"Shirrey?" said a tearful voice.

Jackie was standing inside the classroom. She was trying very hard not to cry.

"Jackie, what's wrong?" exclaimed Shirley. She put down the bud and her scissors. "Are you sick?" Jackie hadn't had trouble in school since those days in the first-grade classroom when everything had been new and scary for her.

"No," replied Jackie, "not sick."

"What, then?" asked Shirley.

"Shirrey, those boys tease me," Jackie began. "They car me yerrow. They car me Srope-eyes. They car me Shorty."

Shirley stood up angrily. "Who? Who calls you those things?" she demanded. (Shirley thought Jackie was beautiful—even if she was short. There was no denying she was short.)

"They are in fifth grade, I think. Big boys."

Shirley paused. She'd wanted to run to whomever had been teasing Jackie and teach them a thing or two. But . . . fifth-grade boys?

"Do you know their names?" asked Shirley.

"Onry first names. Rester and Rance."

"Lester and Lance?" asked Shirley. She hoped Jackie hadn't tried to pronounce their names. That was probably one of the reasons they'd teased her.

Jackie nodded. "Yes. Rester and Rance."

"Jackie," Shirley began, "can you say 'el,' like this?

Listen, little, light, lamb, lump. Say the 'el' part really carefully."

"That is very hard," replied Jackie, "but I try. Risten, ritter—"

"No, *listen, little.*"

Jackie was concentrating so hard that her face was screwed up like an apple doll's. She tried again.

"You know, that was better!" exclaimed Shirley. "It really was!"

"Thank you. But what about Rester and Rance?"

Shirley sighed. "*Lester* and *Lance*," she said under her breath. Then she added more loudly, "Tell me exactly what happened."

"We are in cafeteria for runchtime," said Jackie. "My crass eats at taber next to fifth graders. Mr. Hunt's crass. I am carrying my tray over to taber and I bump into Rester. He says, 'Say excuse me, Srope-eyes.' "

"Slope-eyes?"

Jackie nodded.

"Then what?" asked Shirley.

"So I say 'excuse me' but he won't ret me go by. His friend—Rance—he comes to stand next to him. So I say 'excuse me' to Rance, too. But they do not move. One says, 'How come skin is so yerrow? You are a yerrowbird.' Other one says, 'Go ahead, try to get by, Shorty.' So I try, but Rester knocks tray out of my hands and everything fars on froor."

"Oh, *yeah*?" cried Shirley. Suddenly she didn't care how big or how old Lester and Lance were. She stood up quickly, dumping the scissors and a bottle of Elmer's Glue-All out of her lap. She didn't bother to pick them up. She ran to Jackie, grabbed her by the hand, and pulled her all the way down the hall. When they reached the doors to the cafeteria, she said, "Now you show me Lester and Lance, Jackie. You show them to me this minute."

Jackie looked nervous, but she led Shirley across the cafeteria. When they were standing at the end of a long table, Jackie whispered to Shirley, "These boys. These boys right here are Rester and Rance."

Shirley glared at the two boys sitting at the end of the table. They were calmly eating their lunches.

They were very big.

After a moment, they glanced up and saw Shirley and Jackie looking at them. They grinned at each other.

"Hey, it's Slope-eyes again!" said one of the boys.

Jackie tugged urgently at Shirley's elbow. Then she stood on tiptoe and whispered in Shirley's ear, "That's Rester."

Shirley nodded.

"What are you doing back here, Slope-eyes?" Lester went on.

"You want to buy another lunch—I mean, *runch*?"

asked Lance, grinning a mean grin.

Shirley doubled up her fists and took a step toward the boys.

"So who's this?" Lester asked Jackie. He was pointing to Shirley.

"My sister," Jackie whispered.

"Figures," said Lance. "It figures that the slope-eyes would have a four-eyes for a sister."

Lester and Lance laughed hysterically.

That did it. Shirley had had enough. "I just want to get a few things straight," she said to the boys. "You called Jackie Slope-eyes, right?"

"Yup," said the boys.

"You called her Shorty."

"Right."

"You told her she was yellow."

"Right again."

"You made her drop her lunch tray."

"Her *runch* tray. That's right."

"And you called me a four-eyes."

"You got it."

Shirley nodded. "Just checking," she said.

"How come?" asked Lance.

"Because I don't want to get chocolate pudding on the wrong people," Shirley replied. Then, in one fast movement, she reached out her right hand, picked up Lester's dish of chocolate pudding, and dumped it over his head. At the same time, she reached out her left hand, picked up Lance's dish of pudding, and dumped it over *his* head.

For a moment, no one said a word.

Lester and Lance, with chocolate pudding dripping down their foreheads and into their eyes, just stared at each other.

And Jackie stared at Shirley. Her big sister had done something for her. She had stood up for her. But she had done something wrong, too, hadn't she?

The kids sitting around Lester and Lance looked on in awe.

Out of the corners of her eyes, Shirley tried to glimpse a cafeteria monitor. She didn't see one. She wasn't sure whether to be relieved or worried. On the one hand, she didn't want to get in trouble. On the other hand, Lester was reaching for his mashed potatoes. . . .

"Duck!" Shirley ordered Jackie.

But Jackie knew only one meaning for "duck"—and it didn't have anything to do with crouching down.

The potatoes hit Jackie in the face. She gasped.

Shirley stood up, this time ready to deck Lester— and was hit by Lance's potatoes. She wiped them out of her eyes just in time to see Jackie pick up Lester's carton of milk and pour it over his head. The milk made little white trickles in the chocolate pudding.

"All right, Jackie!" Shirley cried.

"No way!" exclaimed Lester. "No *way!*" He stood up.

The other kids at Lester and Lance's table were no longer just watching. They were laughing and shouting. "Food fight! Food fight!"

"Come on, Jackie, we better get out of here," said Shirley. Now she *did* see a cafeteria monitor, and the monitor was heading their way.

"Not yet," said Jackie through gritted teeth. "One thing more." And she reached for the peas on Lance's plate, picked them up with her hands, and smushed them in his face. "That's for carring me Srope-eyes . . . Rabbit-teeth," she said.

"Oh, boy," muttered Shirley. She was as proud as could be of Jackie, but the cafeteria monitor was closing in. And Lester and Lance looked awfully angry.

Shirley took Jackie by the wrist and pulled her away.

Just in time.

Someone from the other end of Lester and Lance's table had thrown a glob of mashed potatoes at Shirley and Jackie. It missed them.

It hit the cafeteria monitor.

Shirley rushed toward the doorway, yanking Jackie along.

"Come on," said Shirley urgently.

"Where?" puffed Jackie, trying to keep up with her sister.

"Girls' room. We have to get cleaned up before anyone sees us. Oh, I hope there's no one in here."

Shirley barged into the girls' room, then came to a dead stop. She listened. Nothing. The stalls were empty. They were alone.

"Thank goodness," muttered Shirley.

"We get creaned up easy. I mean, easiry," said Jackie. "Nothing on our crothes. Onry on our faces."

"Yeah," agreed Shirley. She turned the water on full blast and reached for a stack of paper towels. Suddenly she burst out laughing.

"What?" asked Jackie.

"Rabbit-teeth!" cried Shirley. "How did you think of that? I didn't even notice that Lance was bucktoothed until you called him that."

"Bucktoothed?" repeated Jackie. "That is how you say it?"

"Yeah, but I like Rabbit-teeth much better."

"I think I read about Rabbit-teeth in a book," said Jackie. She was grinning. "Okay to do that? To put mirk on Rester and peas on Rance?" She began to rinse the green pea goo off of her hands.

"*Very* okay," agreed Shirley. "I mean, Mom and Dad might not think so—if they hear about this— but I'm glad you stuck up for yourself."

"It was fun," said Jackie, wiping at the mashed potatoes that were drying on her cheeks.

"Yeah, it was. . . . Jackie?"

"Yes, Shirrey?"

"I'm really sorry I made fun of you during the spelling bee."

Jackie paused in her washing. "Why *did* you do that?"

"Because, um, I'm not a very good speller," said Shirley slowly. "I was embarrassed when you did better than me. You're my *little* sister. I should be better than you."

Jackie had finished cleaning up. She looked at Shirley seriously. "But you teach me many, many things, Shirrey," she said. "You show me how things work. You exprain about Christmas and Santa Craus. You save me from Rester and Rance. You are very good at those things. Much better than I am. I am onry good at rearning how to read and write and make my math."

"Do your math," Shirley corrected her.

"Do my math," repeated Jackie. "I have to be good at *some*thing. I have to make Mommy and Daddy prease with me."

"Are you kidding?" cried Shirley. "They're pleased with everything you do."

"But when I first come here, I know *nothing*," said Jackie. "You show me everything. I was scared of first grade and my teacher and even Mommy and Daddy. How could they be prease?"

"Well, they were. You learned so fast."

"Maybe...maybe I can teach you some things, Shirrey," said Jackie eagerly. "I teach you sperring words. I show you how to make, I mean, *do* your math."

"I don't know—" began Shirley.

But she didn't get to finish. The door to the girls' room opened then and in walked the cafeteria monitor.

"Ah-*ha*!" she exclaimed.

It was a long time before everything got sorted out. The cafeteria monitor, Mr. Bradley, Mrs. Rockwell, Lester and Lance's teacher, Shirley, Jackie, and Lester and Lance themselves gathered in Mrs. Hillier's office.

"I am in *principar*'s office," Jackie kept whispering to Shirley. She held Shirley's hand tightly.

Mrs. Hillier listened to everything anyone had to say. The only ones who didn't talk were Lester and Lance. Jackie had plenty to say. In fact, Shirley had never heard her say so much.

When everybody was done talking, Mrs. Hillier looked at Lester and Lance sternly. She told them that they would have to stay after school for a week. And that if there was any more trouble between them and Shirley or Jackie, they could expect to stay after school again. Then she dismissed everybody but Shirley and Jackie.

When the three of them were alone in the office, Mrs. Hillier said, "I'm not going to punish you—"

Hurray! thought Shirley.

"—but I have one thing to say. And then I'm going to call your parents."

"Oh, no!" cried Jackie.

"It's all right," Mrs. Hillier said. "I'm going to tell them about the food fight, but only because I want them to know that there was trouble today. What I really want to tell them is that, Jackie, you stood up for yourself, and, Shirley, you stood up for Jackie. They'll be pleased to hear that."

Shirley beamed. Mrs. Hillier was okay.

"I must tell you, though," the principal went on, "that throwing peas and pudding around and pouring milk on people are not the best ways to solve problems. In the future, find a teacher when there's trouble. Or come to me. Understand?"

"Yes," said Shirley.

"Yes," said Jackie.

"Good," said Mrs. Hillier. "You may go now. I'm going to call your parents." She picked up the phone.

Shirley and Jackie left the office. They were still holding hands.

CHAPTER EIGHT: *April*

"Never had a birthday party!" Shirley cried.

"No, never," said Jackie. "I read about them in books. Winnie-the-Pooh had a birthday party, and Dr. Seuss—he writes a big book about having a birthday. And Ritter Bear makes birthday soup on his birthday. The bears get parties, it seems."

"But you have never had a birthday party of your own?" Shirley said again. She just couldn't believe it.

"No," replied Jackie.

"Well, we'll have to do something about that."

It was early April. Jackie's adoption papers showed that her birthday was on April 21. She would turn nine. At school, the Class Artist was hard at work on a bulletin board that showed the playground—and all her classmates playing on the swings, the slide, the seesaws, and the monkey bars. She had glued down cotton balls and coffee grounds again to show the clouds and the earth.

But now, Jackie's birthday had become more important than the bulletin board.

"Mom," said Shirley right after she had found out that Jackie had never had a party, "we have to fix this. We have to do something really terrific. She has to have a *real* birthday party, to make up for all the ones she missed."

"What do you suggest?" asked Mrs. Basini.

Shirley glanced around, as if Jackie might be listening, even though she had made her mother come into the den with her and had closed the door for privacy.

"I suggest we do *everything*," Shirley replied seriously. "We invite her entire class, plus Sessie and Joan. We get a clown or a magician. We play pin-the-tail-on-the-donkey and musical chairs and have a peanut hunt. Cake and ice cream and presents, of course. Then maybe rent some cartoons to play on the VCR so we can calm the kids down before they go home. Oh, and goody bags. We can't forget goody bags. And prizes and favors and balloons and party poppers and—"

Mrs. Basini began to laugh. "You've already got everything figured out!" she said.

"But what do you think, Mom?"

"I think it's a lovely idea. Why don't you plan the party and give it yourself?"

"*Me?*" cried Shirley. It seemed as if her mother always expected more of Shirley than Shirley thought she could handle.

"I'll be glad to help you," Mrs. Basini went on. "So will Dad. But it sounds like you're halfway there already."

"Well . . . okay," said Shirley. "I'll try it."

Shirley hesitantly set to work. She went to the cabinet where the paper and crayons and Magic Markers and other art supplies were stored. She had to get started on the invitations and send them out. It was already Wednesday, April 2. Jackie's birthday was in less than three weeks. Shirley didn't want any of Jackie's friends making other plans for Monday, April 21. She wanted them all to come to Jackie's party.

Shirley also wanted to make the party invitations herself, but she felt pressed for time. She could never make each one separately. It would take far too long. So Shirley decided to draw a smiling clown holding a bunch of balloons and copy it in the library on the Xerox machine the next day. Then all she would have to do was color in a few things on each invitation, and they would be ready to mail out.

When Shirley's clown was finished, she was pleased. She added his bunch of balloons. In one balloon she wrote the date of the party, in another the

time, in a third the place. Under the picture she wrote
in big letters:

ITS JakcIes BiRTHDaY !!!

The invitations were copied, colored, stamped, and
mailed by Friday.

Shirley turned her attention to other things.

"How am I going to remember everything we need
to buy?" she asked her father nervously the next day.
"We need so much stuff—crepe paper, balloons,
favors, candy, hats, ice cream, icing for the cake, cake
decorations. Even more. What if I forget something?"

"Why don't you try making lists?" suggested her
father. "Make one list for food, one for decorations,
one for the table, and so on."

"Oh," said Shirley. "Good idea. Thanks."

So she began making lists.

And then she began looking for a clown or a magician to entertain at the party. Her parents helped her.
Shirley made lots of phone calls, but she couldn't decide between Moonstar the magician and Ho-Ho the
clown.

On Saturday, April 12, Shirley was still trying to
make up her mind. She was sitting in the den looking
at two leaflets. One was an ad for Moonstar. The
other was an ad for Ho-Ho. They both sounded like
fun. Moonstar would pull candy bars from his hat and

give them to the guests. He would let the birthday girl be his assistant. On the other hand, Ho-Ho would—

Ding-dong!

"I'll get it!" shouted Shirley. She dropped the leaflets and ran to the front hall.

When she opened the door, her eyes widened in surprise. Standing on the stoop were two girls from Jackie's class. They were very dressed up—party dresses, patent leather shoes, ribbons in their hair. And each one was carrying a present.

"Yes?" said Shirley, puzzled.

"We're here for the party," said one of the girls, whose name was Stephanie. Stephanie pushed past Shirley. Her friend followed. "Jackie?" called Stephanie.

"You guys are—" Shirley began, closing the door. But before the door was closed all the way, the bell rang again.

Shirley flung the door open. This time two boys from Jackie's class were on the stoop. They were holding gifts, too. Beyond them, Shirley caught sight of Sessie and Joan. They were crossing the yard, presents in hand.

"What's going on?" Shirley asked. She wasn't speaking to anybody in particular, so nobody answered her.

The boys, Sessie, and Joan went inside.

"Shirley?" called Mrs. Basini.

Shirley turned around and went back in the house. The six children were standing in the front hall with Mr. and Mrs. Basini. Jackie was coming down the stairs.

"What's going on?" asked Mrs. Basini.

"That's what I want to know," Shirley replied. "These kids keep coming over with presents."

"Hi, Jackie!" Stephanie cried suddenly. "Happy birthday!" Jackie had entered the hall, and Stephanie thrust a present toward her. The other kids did the same.

"Today is my birthday party?" Jackie asked incredulously.

"Well, it's not supposed to be," said Shirley.

The doorbell rang again and three more kids arrived.

"I just love Saturday birthdays," said Sessie. "People with Saturday birthdays are lucky ducks."

"But Jackie's birthday isn't today," Shirley told her.

"It isn't? The invitation said April twelfth."

Shirley looked helplessly at her parents.

"Oh, Shirley," said Mrs. Basini, sounding disappointed, "you must have written twelve instead of twenty-one. You switched around the one and the two."

"No," whispered Shirley. "No, I couldn't have. That was so stupid!" Shirley felt tears pricking at her eyes.

She looked at her mother. Her mother looked at her father. Her father looked thoughtfully at the party that was taking place in the hallway.

"Well," said Mr. Basini, "there's nothing to do but let the fun start!"

"But, Dad!" cried Shirley. She took her father's arm and pulled him away from the kids. "We can't have the party today! There's no cake. There aren't any decorations or prizes. I haven't even decided between Moonstar and Ho-Ho."

"I know, peanut," her father said gently. "We have to do something, though. All the kids are being dropped off. Their parents won't be back for two hours. We'll just play some games, and invite them to return on the twenty-first."

"What a stupid mistake I made," said Shirley, and she could feel the tears starting again.

"Don't feel too bad," said her father. "Everyone makes careless mistakes."

"But I make the most of anybody. If I don't pay attention to every little thing all the time—this is what happens." Shirley swept her arm toward the front hall, where two more kids were arriving.

Her father gave her a hug. Then he said, "Come on. We have work to do."

The party guests kept arriving. When every kid from Jackie's class had shown up, Shirley said, "I have an announcement to make." She climbed onto a chair in the living room and stood on it unsteadily. Piled on the couch next to her were Jackie's presents. Jackie and her friends looked at Shirley expectantly.

"My announcement is this," said Shirley. "Um . . . I made—I made a mistake. Jackie's party isn't supposed to be today. It'll be in a week and a half. We don't have any cake or ice cream—"

"Oh," groaned the guests.

Shirley glanced at her parents who were standing in the doorway to the living room. Her father nodded encouragingly. He actually looked sort of proud.

"And," Shirley went on, "we don't have a clown or a magician or decorations or prizes. *But* we can play some games today, and when you come back on the twenty-first, we're going to have one super-duper party. I promise."

"Yea!" cried the kids.

"Can you come back?" asked Shirley.

Jackie's friends said that they'd have to ask their parents, but most of them thought they could come back.

"Great," said Shirley. She jumped off the chair. Then she said to Jackie, "I'm really sorry. But you know what you could do now?"

"What?" asked Jackie.

"If you wanted to, you could open your presents. We'll hardly have time for that at your real party."

"Goody," said Jackie, "we can pray with new toys, too."

Jackie began opening her gifts while Mr. Basini ran to the store and bought two boxes of Popsicles. When he returned, Jackie was still working on the presents. She wasn't even halfway finished.

Shirley tiptoed over to her father and whispered, "I have never seen anyone open presents as slowly as Jackie. She peels off each piece of tape, never rips the paper, and then she folds the paper up and saves it in a pile."

The kids didn't seem to mind, though. Half of them were watching Jackie's delicate package-opening process. The other half were playing with the presents she'd already opened.

Shirley sat down next to her sister. She was just about to say, "Maybe you could speed things up a little," when Jackie paused in her work.

"Shirrey," she said, "I'm grad you made birthday mistake."

"You are?" Shirley replied.

Jackie nodded. "This is fun. We have two parties. A ritter one today on my not-birthday, and then a big one on my birthday. Thank you."

Shirley hugged Jackie. "You're welcome. And thank *you*."

"For what?"

"For being glad about this mess I made."

Jackie smiled. Then she added, "It is a nice mess. I rike it."

Jackie's present opening went on for twenty more minutes. Then, because the weather was nice, Mrs. Basini shooed everyone outdoors. She passed out the Popsicles. When they were eaten, Shirley led the guests in Simon says and red light, green light, and Mother, may I?

Before she knew it, the parents started arriving to pick up their children. As they left, Shirley and her parents reminded each of them to come back on April 21.

One week and two days later, Jackie Basini turned nine.

"Happy birthday! Happy birthday!" Shirley shouted as she threw the baseball alarm clock at the wall. "It's your birthday, Jackie! Your *real* birthday."

Jackie smiled sleepily. "Today I have birthday party, just like Pooh Bear," she said, and yawned.

"Yeah, and what a party. Boy, will I have a lot to do when I get home this afternoon. I wonder if Mom would let me skip school today so I could—"

"No way," said Mrs. Basini's voice.

"Darn," said Shirley.

Mr. and Mrs. Basini entered the girls' room.

"Happy birthday, honey," they said to Jackie. They kissed Jackie and Shirley good morning. And Mrs. Basini added to Shirley, "I am so proud of the way you worked on this party."

"You *are?*" said Shirley. "Thanks!" She grinned.

"But it doesn't require time off from school. I'll give you a hand with things when you come home. And I'll set the table this morning."

"Okay," said Shirley. She didn't want to spoil the morning with an argument.

When school was over that day, Shirley and Jackie walked home together. Shirley was positive she hadn't paid attention the entire day. She knew this because at two-fifteen, Mr. Bradley had shouted, "Shirley Basini, you haven't paid attention the entire day!"

Shirley couldn't help it. She was far too excited about the party. She had a million details to think of.

When she and Jackie got home, Shirley hustled Jackie up to their room and told her to change into her party clothes. "And then stay here till it's time for the party, okay?" said Shirley. "I'll come get you. I don't want you to see anything downstairs. I want you to be surprised."

"Okay," replied Jackie.

Shirley didn't know exactly what Jackie was expecting, but when the guests started to arrive later, and Shirley led Jackie down to the party, Jackie nearly fainted.

She looked around at the living room, which was decorated with crepe paper and balloons. It was set up like a little theater so the guests could watch Moonstar the magician perform. Then she peeked into the dining room. Streamers crisscrossed the ceiling. A huge bunch of pink balloons hung over Jackie's place at the head of the table. The table was set with teddy-bear plates and cups and napkins. Party favors and candy and goody bags were at every place.

Jackie drew in her breath. "*Oh*," was all she could say.

"Do you like your birthday party?" Shirley asked her.

"It is perfect," whispered Jackie, her eyes shining.

Everything about the party was new for Jackie. She had read about magicians, but she hadn't seen a real one. She gasped when Moonstar began pulling candy bars out of his hat. Later, she played her very first games ever of pin-the-tail-on-the-donkey and musical chairs. When it was time to sit down at the table, Sessie had to show Jackie how to pop her popper, how to blow her blower, and even how to wear her hat.

And then the cake was served. Shirley carried it into the dining room. The lights had been dimmed. The room was lit only by the glow of the candles. Very softly, the guests began to sing "Happy Birthday."

Jackie could only stare. Shirley thought her sister was going to cry. She set the cake in front of her. "Make a wish and blow out the candles," she said.

"Make a wish?" Jackie repeated.

"For anything you want," added Sessie.

Jackie frowned. She closed her eyes. Then she said loudly, "I wish for two birthday parties every year."

"No, no!" cried Sessie. "Your wish is supposed to be a secret!"

"If it is secret, how does anybody know what I want?" asked Jackie sensibly. Then she blew out the candles.

When she was done, she looked up at Shirley who was standing by her side, holding the cake cutter. "Thank you," she said, "this is best birthday of my rife."

CHAPTER NINE: *May*

In May, the Class Artist started a new bulletin board. Shirley had had a hard time thinking of a theme for it. Some months had been easy because of holidays— Thanksgiving and Valentine's Day. Others had been easy because she could show the changing seasons. But May was tough. Shirley had already made a spring bulletin board, and she was saving the summer scene for her grand finale in June. The only important May holiday was Memorial Day.

Boring, thought Shirley.

At first.

But when she couldn't come up with any ideas for May, she decided to find out what Memorial Day was all about. She had to look it up in three different books. Mr. Soderman helped her. It was, she learned, a day set aside to honor servicemen who had passed away.

It was a patriotic holiday.

Shirley thought and thought. At last she made a banner that she stretched across the top of the bulletin board from one end to the other. Her banner read: MAY 30 MEMRAIL DAY. Mr. Bradley looked at it. He helped Shirley to fix the spelling. When the banner was in place, Shirley turned the rest of the bulletin board into one gigantic American flag, with the right number of stars and stripes.

It was very catchy. And, thought Shirley, it *said* something. It was important. Furthermore, most of Shirley's classmates didn't know that Memorial Day meant anything more than a day off from school. Mr. Bradley asked Shirley to stand up and explain what it really meant.

Shirley was proud. Another good bulletin board, Mr. Bradley was pleased with her—and in five weeks, school would let out for the summer.

One day in the Resource Room, Mr. Soderman asked Shirley, "What are you going to do this summer?"

"Swim," replied Shirley. "Ride my bicycle. Teach Jackie to swim and ride a bike. And, oh, I guess... read," she added softly.

"What was that?"

"Read. There's a contest at the public library this summer. You keep track of how many books you read, and at the end of the summer, the kids who have read the most, win prizes."

"Well, that sounds like fun," said Mr. Soderman. He smiled at Shirley. "I'm glad you found out you like to read after all."

"Yeah," said Shirley. "Me, too." Reading still wasn't *easy*, she thought. But it was usually fun.

Shirley had been working hard in the Resource Room. She had been working hard in Mr. Bradley's room. She had stayed in her seat and hadn't made jokes or called out or distracted the kids around her. Everyone seemed pleased with Shirley.

So Shirley was surprised when Mr. Bradley called her to his desk at the end of school one day and handed her a note in an envelope. "This is for your parents," he said. "Will you be sure to give it to them?"

Shirley nodded. "Yes," she said, feeling worried.

Shirley walked home from school by herself that afternoon. She knew that no one would be at her house when she got there. Her father was at work, her mother was busy with Meals-on-Wheels, and Jackie had been invited to Joan's.

As Shirley walked along, she thought about the envelope that was in her schoolbag. Her stomach began to feel funny. She reached into the bag and pulled the envelope out. It was addressed to Mr. and Mrs. Basini. Shirley turned it over.

The envelope wasn't sealed!

Quick as a flash, Shirley dropped her things on the ground. She sat down in the middle of the sidewalk and opened the envelope. Inside was a typewritten letter.

"Dear Mr. and Mrs. Basini," it began, "I would like to recommend that Shirley attend summer school for eight weeks during the months of July and August. This will be necessary in order for her to enter the fifth grade this fall."

What did that mean? That if Shirley *didn't* go to summer school, she'd have to stay back? She and Jackie would both be in fourth grade then, only Jackie would be in the smart class. And Shirley would probably still have to go to the Resource Room.

The letter went on and on, but Shirley didn't bother to read it. She'd read enough.

Tears welled up in Shirley's eyes. Oh, her parents were going to be so upset. Especially her mother. Joe had never had to go to summer school. Jackie would certainly never have to go. And not even a year ago Jackie couldn't even speak English! Who had helped Jackie learn to speak? Who had helped her with her reading and spelling when she was in the first-grade room? Who had told her about *Henry and Ribsy*? Shir-

ley, that's who. And now *Shirley* had to go to summer
school. Face it, she thought, Jackie and Joe were just
plain smarter than she was.

Shirley couldn't imagine what her parents would
do or say when they read the note from Mr. Bradley.
But she knew how they would feel. Disappointed.

Shirley's tears spilled over and ran down her
cheeks. Didn't anybody understand how hard she'd
tried that year? She stood up, stuffing the note in her
schoolbag. Then she walked slowly home.

By the time she'd reached her house, she'd made a
decision.

She was going to run away.

It was the only thing to do. Then her parents
wouldn't have to worry about her anymore.

Shirley went to her room and found her suitcase.
She threw some clothes in it. She threw her baseball
alarm clock in it. She threw her good shoes in it.
Then she opened her bank and emptied out her
money. She counted it three times. She had eleven
dollars and sixty-five cents. She stuffed the money in
the pocket of her jeans.

Shirley carried her suitcase downstairs. When she
reached the kitchen, she sat down at the table with a
blank piece of paper in front of her. She thought and
thought. After a long time, she wrote:

pear FaimlY:
I Have run away. I Hav To go To sumgr sHool. Im verry sorry. Im sorry I made You DisaPerntened. You will Be Better oF witHout me.
Yours TurLY,
SHirleY (You'r DoTTer anD SisTer)

She placed her note on top of Mr. Bradley's letter, and left them both on the table.

Shirley lugged her suitcase outside and down the driveway. The suitcase certainly was heavy. Maybe she shouldn't have packed her good shoes. And she wasn't sure she'd need the alarm clock. But it was too late to go back now. Someone might come home and catch her.

It wasn't easy, but Shirley managed to get her suitcase all the way to the playground by the shopping center. Sometimes she had to drag it. The dragging made long scratch marks on the bottom. Oh, well, what difference did it make? Her parents would never see her or the suitcase again.

Shirley sat on the bottom of the slide until the sun began to sink behind the trees. Where would she spend the night? she wondered. Where did people go when they ran away? Did they sleep in the woods? Shirley didn't want to do that. And she couldn't take the bus to Joe or any of her relatives. They'd send her right back home.

Shirley's stomach began to growl. She should have packed some food. And where *was* she going to sleep? Shirley hadn't spent the night in too many places besides her own bed. She had slept over at friends' houses a few times. She and her parents had spent several nights in hotels. Once, her family had camped out in Maine. And once she had slept in the tree house. . . . The tree house! *That*'s where Shirley could sleep. What a brilliant idea! She could spend the night there and worry about where to run away to the next day.

Shirley walked back to her neighborhood as fast as she could, which wasn't very fast. Her suitcase felt heavier with every step she took. When she reached the house that was two doors away from her own, she crept around the side. Then she cut through the yards to the Basinis' property.

She paused under the tree house. How was she going to get her suitcase up there? She thought and thought. There was no way to do it. She'd have to hide it somewhere. Maybe the garage, if no one was home yet.

Shirley studied the back of her house. A light was on in her bedroom. Jackie had probably come home, but not her parents. If her parents had come home, they would have found the notes. They'd be looking for Shirley. They'd be calling and shouting. Maybe even crying.

Shirley smiled. She was a pretty good detective. Too bad she couldn't tell that to Mr. Bradley.

But Mr. and Mrs. Basini would be home soon, so Shirley would have to hurry. She dragged her suitcase into the garage and shoved it under the shelves that her mother had built to hold tools and flowerpots and empty jars and all the things the Basinis didn't need but couldn't bear to throw away. And there, on the shelf just above her suitcase, was the box with the baby minder in it—the baby minder her mother had bought when she thought Jackie was going to be a three-year-old instead of an eight-year-old.

It was the sight of the baby minder that gave Shirley the best idea she had ever had. She only hoped she had enough time to pull it off. And that she could be quiet enough to pull it off.

Without a second thought, she opened the box, grabbed the baby minder, and checked to make sure it had batteries. Then she tiptoed into her kitchen, set the monitor on the counter, plugged it in behind the dish towels hanging on the rack, and tiptoed back out, with the intercom in her hand.

Not a moment too soon.

Shirley was just climbing the last rung of the ladder to the tree house when a car pulled into the driveway. She scrambled inside, scooted behind the front wall, and peered out through a knothole. It was her mother's car.

Shirley flicked on the intercom. She turned the volume up high. Soon she heard a door slam, and a faint voice, which was her mother's, calling, "Girls! Shirley? Jackie? I'm home."

Then for a few seconds, Shirley heard only a scuffling sound. She guessed it was Jackie coming downstairs. Or her mother putting her things away.

Then silence.

Suddenly a voice blasted over the intercom. "Jackie!" exclaimed Mrs. Basini. "Did you see this?" (Shirley hurriedly turned the volume down.)

Jackie and Mrs. Basini must be in the kitchen. Perfect, thought Shirley.

"See what?" Jackie replied.

"This note from Shirley." Mrs. Basini read the note to Jackie.

"Exprain 'run away,' prease," Shirley heard Jackie say.

"Oh, honey, not right now. Have you seen Shirley this afternoon?"

"No. I spend afternoon at Joan's."

"But Shirley was in school today, wasn't she?"

"Oh, yes," said Jackie.

"Well, that's something. You're sure Shirley isn't at home?"

"No. She is not here."

"Okay. I've got to call Daddy."

In the quiet that followed, Shirley heard another car pull into her driveway. She looked through the knothole. It was her father.

And at that moment, Jackie said, "Mommy, I think Daddy is home."

"Oh, thank heavens," said Mrs. Basini.

Pause.

Shirley heard faint voices that grew louder.

". . . what I found!" her mother was crying.

"What's this?" asked Mr. Basini.

Papers rustled.

"It's from Mr. Bradley," said Shirley's mother.

Mumble, mumble. "Oh, *summer* school," said Mr. Basini. "That's what she meant."

"Exprain 'summer schoo,' prease," said Jackie desperately.

"Not right now," Shirley's parents replied at the same time.

"Oh, what are we going to *do*?" (That was Mrs. Basini.) "Maybe we ought to call the police."

"Porice!" exclaimed Jackie. "But why?"

"Because your sister is missing, that's why."

Shirley listened and listened. Her parents were talking a mile a minute. They decided not to call the police just then. First they were going to call her friends and Joe, and then drive around the neighborhood.

Shirley began to feel puzzled. She had *wanted* to see what her parents would do when they found her notes. That was why she had set up the baby minder, of course. But why didn't her parents sound angry or disappointed? All Shirley could hear in their voices was worry and fear. They hadn't said a thing about how awful summer school was.

I should go back, thought Shirley. I should go back right now. Even if they do care about summer school a little bit, I should go back before they start driving around. And certainly before they call the police.

Shirley wasn't in trouble, then. But she would be if the police started looking for her and found her in the tree house. How was she supposed to go home, though? She couldn't just walk in the front door and say, "Hi. Here I am. Sorry I ran away."

Maybe another note would do the trick. Shirley's mind began clicking away as fast as when she had a good idea for a bulletin board. When her plan was worked out, she picked up the intercom and climbed carefully out of the tree house. She kept the intercom on, the volume low. She paused just outside the garage, near the trash cans. From the sound of things inside, Mrs. Basini was on the phone with Erin's mother. Jackie and her father were looking through an address book, making a list of other people to call.

Shirley turned the intercom off. Silently, she removed the lid from one of the trash cans. Pew. The smell was terrible. Shirley set the intercom down so she could hold her nose with one hand and look for a scrap of paper with the other. When she found one, she put the lid on the can again and took the intercom and the paper into the garage with her. Then she returned the intercom to its box. She searched the junk shelves until she found a pencil.

Shirley settled herself on the floor and wrote:

> Dear Faimly:
> I Have come Home. are you made at mg, I Hope not. IF you are not made and You really want me Back come To THe garage Im in THe garage.
> Yours Turly,
> SHirley

She tiptoed around to the front of the house and placed the note on the front stoop where it would be easy to see. Then she rang the doorbell and ran back to the garage as fast as her legs could carry her.

When Mr. and Mrs. Basini and Jackie dashed into the garage a few moments later, they found Shirley sitting on her suitcase, looking as if she had just come home.

Mrs. Basini ran to her and gathered her in her arms. "Oh, thank goodness you came back! I don't know what we'd have done if—" She broke off.

"Mom!" Shirley exclaimed. "Are you *crying*?"

"A little."

Shirley looked up at her father and Jackie. They were wiping tears away, too.

"I guess you're not mad," Shirley ventured.

"Well, maybe just slightly," replied her father. "You scared us to death. Besides, running away is never the answer to a problem."

"You must have felt like there was nothing else you could do, though," said Mrs. Basini. She let go of Shirley, and the four Basinis walked into the house. They sat down around the kitchen table.

Shirley glanced nervously at the counter where the baby minder monitor was hidden. She'd have to be sure to put it away before it was discovered. And at some point she'd have to show her parents the damaged suitcase. But not just then. That could wait.

"You're right. I *didn't* know what else to do," Shirley admitted. "And, um, I felt ashamed."

"Ashamed? Why?" asked her father.

"Because!" cried Shirley. (Wasn't it obvious?) "Only kids who get bad grades have to go to summer school."

"I don't agree," said Mr. Basini, "and I should know. I'm a teacher. Also, I spoke to Mr. Bradley." (When had that happened? wondered Shirley. Probably when she was in the garage writing the second note.) "He said he wants you to go to summer school because you've improved so much this year. If you hadn't done so well, summer school wouldn't be any help. Then you'd have to stay back."

"Really?" exclaimed Shirley.

"Really," said Mrs. Basini. "And guess who your summer-school teacher is going to be?"

"Who?"

"Mr. Soderman."

"All *right*!" Shirley felt relieved and proud and happy.

Her parents grinned at her.

But Jackie looked frustrated. "Would someone, *prease*," she said, "exprain now 'run away' and 'summer schoo.' "

Shirley smiled. "I'll explain," she told her parents.

CHAPTER TEN: *June*

Shirley stood back from the bulletin board. She looked at it proudly. The June bulletin board, she decided, was the best of the year. It was a summer scene. She'd thought about it hard. And she'd planned it carefully. What, Shirley had asked herself, was one of the best things about summer? The answer was easy—swimming. But how could she make realistic water? Shirley didn't want her swimming pool to be just a piece of blue construction paper on the board. No, it had to be more special than that.

Shirley worked on the rest of the scene first. She made a couple of lifeguards to watch over the pool. She made some swimmers and sunbathers, a brilliant sun, and some puffy clouds. She made beach balls and flippers and rafts.

When she couldn't put it off any longer, she tackled the water. She experimented with paper and paint and even papier-mâché. At last she discovered something wonderful—tinfoil. She colored it blue with a fat Magic Marker and crinkled it a little. It made wavy, amazing-looking water! Shirley glued it to the board. Then she added the other figures she had made.

Once again, her classmates were impressed. Especially with the water. Shirley was satisfied. Her final bulletin board was a success, and school was nearly over. She still faced summer school, but that didn't seem so bad anymore. And Jackie was jealous! She wanted to go to school year round, too. Like Shirley.

One day, when the end of fourth grade was just a week and a half away, Mr. Bradley gave Shirley's class an assignment.

"I want you to write about 'family,' " he said.

And that's all he would say, except that he wanted each composition to be two to three pages long. They were due in a week.

"Do you want us to write about *our* families?" asked Ned Hernandez.

Mr. Bradley shrugged.

"Do you want us to write about the *people* in our families?" asked Jason Rice.

Mr. Bradley shrugged again.

Shirley had about a million questions, but she didn't raise her hand. What was the point, if Mr. Bradley was just going to stand there and shrug? She took the problem to Mr. Soderman in the Resource Room that afternoon.

"What do you think a family is?" Mr. Soderman asked Shirley.

"A mom and a dad and their kids," Shirley replied. She paused. "No, that's not right. Some parents get divorced or die. The people who are left are still a family. And Jackie's in my family, but she's not my parents' kid. Not a real one, anyway."

Mr. Soderman's eyes traveled across the room. Shirley followed his gaze—to the dictionary.

"Oh!" she exclaimed. "We'll see what the dictionary says. It's always right."

After Shirley had looked up "family" in the dictionary, though, she said, "There are nine different definitions in there, and I don't really like any of them. The one about a family being all the members of a household is close, I guess. But it leaves out relatives who don't live in your house. Like my brother Joe. And my grandparents. The definitions about parents and children and relatives—they're not quite right either. They leave out Jackie."

"There you go," said Mr. Soderman.

"Huh?"

"I think you've got your composition. You have

very strong opinions about the meaning of 'family.' "

"Yeah," said Shirley slowly, "I do."

"Well, why don't you get started?" suggested Mr. Soderman.

"*Now?*" replied Shirley in dismay. The composition wasn't due for days. Besides, she was in the middle of a terrific Beverly Cleary book, *Dear Mr. Henshaw*.

"There's no time like the present," Mr. Soderman replied.

"Okay," said Shirley with a sigh.

She placed a pad of paper in front of her. She poised a pencil over it. She wrote,

a Faimly is what you make it.

"I like that," Mr. Soderman commented.

Shirley nodded thoughtfully. Then she continued with her work. a Faimly is a grop of people who love each other and help each other. Maybe their relatip, Maybe their no t.

Suddenly Shirley had an awful lot to say on the subject. Mr. Soderman was right. She did have strong opinions about the meaning of "family." Shirley filled two and three-quarters pages before it was time for her to go back to Mr. Bradley's room.

"That's wonderful," Mr. Soderman told her with a

smile. "You have a really terrific rough draft here."

"Rough draft?" Shirley repeated. "What do you mean?"

"I mean your first try at the composition. You wrote it off the top of your head—very quickly. Now it needs some polishing and fixing up. Afterward, I'll show you which words you've misspelled and the places where the punctuation is wrong. Then you can correct everything."

"Oh," said Shirley with a groan, "I thought I was finished."

Far from it. Over the next few days, Shirley rewrote her composition three times. She was surprised. She did find things she wanted to change or fix, or make clearer or funnier or sadder. When her composition said just what she wanted it to say, Mr. Soderman helped her with the spelling and punctuation. Not that he did anything *for* her. He sent Shirley to the dictionary fifteen different times, to look up words she hadn't spelled right.

When Shirley finally gave her paper to Mr. Bradley, she breathed a sigh of relief.

Then she forgot about the assignment.

"No more school! No more books! No more teachers' dirty looks!" sang Shirley.

It was the last day of fourth grade. Shirley had been waiting weeks to teach that poem to Jackie. She recited it for her as they walked to school in the morning.

"Now you try it," Shirley said.

"No more schoo! No more books! No more teachers' dirty . . . dirty *looks*!" Jackie cried triumphantly.

"What did you say?" Shirley asked her sister in amazement. "Say that last part again."

"No more teachers' dirty *looks*! I can say it, Shir-Shir*ley*!"

"You sure can! That's great!"

Shirley and Jackie skipped on to school. Jackie made up a new poem. "Lester and Lance! Lester and Lance! They lost their stinky underpants!"

Shirley dissolved in laughter.

The last day of school was one of the days of the year that Shirley liked best. There was no work to be done—just desks to be cleaned out, old papers to be handed back, and maybe games to be played or even a party to be held.

Mr. Bradley got down to business right away.

"Desks first," he announced. "I want them cleaned inside and out."

Shirley's desk was stuffed. It was so full that she dragged the trash can up to it and just kept pulling paper out and throwing it away. She did find two interesting things that she kept, however—a whole pack of strawberry bubble gum and her squirting ring. It was the ring she had brought to school on the first day of fourth grade. That had been ten months ago. It felt like ten years.

When Shirley was done cleaning her desk, she filled her ring with water.

"Hey, Ned," she said, holding out her hand, "look."

Ned was scrubbing the top of his desk with Fantastik. He glanced up. "Oh," he said, "your squirting ring. You found it. Here. Squirt some water on my desk, would you? It needs it."

"Aw, you're no fun," said Shirley.

Ned crossed his eyes at her.

By the afternoon, Mr. Bradley's classroom looked clean—and empty. Shirley's bulletin board masterpiece was gone. The walls were almost bare. Shirley thought the room seemed sad.

She was glad when Mr. Bradley said, "Before the bell rings, class, we have one special, last-day thing to do."

Good, thought Shirley. She hoped it would be a party.

Mr. Bradley held up a bunch of papers. "Remember your compositions about families?" he said.

A few kids groaned. They hadn't remembered. Shirley was one of the groaners. This was the last thing she needed—one final bad grade to show her parents. What a way to end the year.

"I didn't grade your papers," Mr. Bradley said. (He didn't?) "But," he went on, "they were so good that I've decided to award prizes to five of you. Some of you put a lot of thought and effort into your compositions, and I'd like the rest of the class to hear what you wrote. So we'll spend this last half hour awarding prizes and reading the winning papers.

"The prizes will be given for the best organized composition, the most thoughtful, the most original, the best written, and finally the all-around best composition."

Shirley and her classmates sat up a little straighter. This was pretty exciting. And it was unexpected. Mr. Bradley had never given out prizes. What would they be?

"The prize for the best organized composition," Mr. Bradley said, "goes to Patrick Blake. His prize is a copy of *Stuart Little* by E. B. White."

Shirley clapped her hands as Patrick walked to the front of the room to get his brand-new paperback book and his composition.

Books! Shirley thought excitedly. The prizes were books! Maybe Patrick would lend *Stuart Little* to her. She hadn't read that yet. She sat back to see what the other books would be.

Mr. Bradley called three more students to the front of the room and gave out three more books: for the most thoughtful composition, *A Bear Called Padding-ton;* for the most original, *The Secret Garden;* for the best written, *Winnie-the-Pooh.*

One more prize to go.

"And finally," Mr. Bradley said, a huge grin on his face, "the prize for the all-around best composition goes to . . . Shirley Basini."

Shirley knew she hadn't heard right. How could she have? A prize for *her?* A *school* prize?

"Come on up, Shirley," said her teacher, "your composition was wonderful."

Shirley got slowly out of her seat and walked to Mr. Bradley. He handed her composition to her. And then he gave her a copy of *Henry and Ribsy.*

Shirley could only stare at it. When she finally looked up at Mr. Bradley, she whispered, "Thank you."

"You're welcome," he replied. "You deserve it. Good work, Shirley."

Shirley knew that she read her composition to the class that afternoon. She knew that they clapped. But by the time she and Jackie got home after school, she barely remembered any of it. All she could think of was her paper with the big gold star on the top. And *Henry and Ribsy.* Her very own copy.

"Jackie," she said, "can you keep a secret?"

"Yes," replied her sister. "I like secrets. I can keep one."

"Good. Let's not say anything about my prize for a while. Let's wait until after dinner. Then I can show Mom and Dad the book and the composition. I can surprise them."

"Okay," agreed Jackie.

Waiting until after dinner wasn't easy. Shirley kept wanting to blurt out her good news, especially when her mother said, "Did anything interesting happen on your last day of school, girls?"

Shirley and Jackie looked at each other over the tops of their glasses of milk. "Nope," Shirley managed to reply after she'd swallowed.

Then Joe phoned. He was still at his college, but he would be home very soon. Shirley wanted *badly* to tell him about her prize—but she wanted to tell her parents first.

"Mom? Dad?" Shirley said when the Basinis had finished talking to Joe. "Can you come into the living room? I have something to show you."

Jackie began jumping up and down. "It is exciting!" she cried. "It is very exciting!"

Shirley told her parents and Jackie to sit on the couch. When they were ready, she made her entrance, carrying the composition and the book. She held up the composition so that everyone could see the star.

"I won a prize in school today," she announced, "for writing the all-around best composition about families. And Mr. Bradley gave me a prize." She produced *Henry and Ribsy*, which she'd been hiding behind her back.

"Shirley! How wonderful!" exclaimed her mother.

"Congratulations, peanut!" said her father.

Her parents and Jackie were smiling. They asked lots of questions. Then Mrs. Basini said, "Would you read us your composition, honey? We'd love to hear it."

"Of course," Shirley replied importantly. And she began reading.

"A family is what you make it. A family is a group of people who love each other and help each other. Maybe they're related, maybe they're not." She read on and on—about people in a family sometimes not being together but always feeling together, and the part about a family opening up, making room for a new member, and then closing around the new member to include her. "That's you, Jackie," Shirley added.

Then Shirley read the parts about things that had happened after Joe had gone away and after Jackie had arrived. Once she'd started writing, she'd remembered lots of details. "Put them in," Mr. Soderman had urged her. "They'll make your composition come alive." Shirley had followed his advice.

When Shirley finished reading, she was surprised to find that her mother was crying.

"Why?" asked Shirley, startled.

"Because what you wrote was lovely and insightful. And, honestly, you do have an eye for detail and a good memory. You're like a sponge, soaking up everything around you."

A sponge! Mrs. Basini had called Shirley a sponge —just like Jackie!

Shirley beamed.

Then her father said, "We were going to wait a few weeks to give you this news—to take the edge off your first morning at summer school—but I think we'll tell you now. *We* have a surprise for *you*, Shirley."

"You do?" asked Shirley.

"Yes. We've signed you up for art classes this summer. You did such a good job with the bulletin boards all year, that we thought—"

"Oh, *thank* you!" Shirley cried, before her father could finish. "Thank you, thank you, thank you!"

"Don't worry, Jackie," Mr. Basini went on, "we didn't forget you. There's a special program at the school library in July and August. We signed you up for that."

"Oh, goody! Thank you, Daddy! Thank you, Mommy!"

"You know what?" Shirley said suddenly. "I wasn't sure what fourth grade was going to be like. I thought it was going to be terrible."

"And I wasn't sure what America would be like," said Jackie.

"But we survived, didn't we?" Shirley said to her. "We both survived. I think the Basini sisters can do just about anything."

"Yes," replied Jackie. "Even beat Lester and Lance."

And Shirley and Jackie walked upstairs to their bedroom singing, "Lester and Lance! Lester and Lance! They lost their stinky underpants!"

About the Author

ANN M. MARTIN grew up in Princeton, New Jersey, and is a graduate of Smith College. Her other Apple paperbacks are *Ten Kids, No Pets; With You and Without You; Me and Katie (the Pest); Stage Fright; Inside Out; Bummer Summer;* and the books in THE BABY-SITTERS CLUB series and the BABY-SITTERS LITTLE SISTER series.

Ms. Martin lives in New York City with her cat, Mouse. She likes ice cream and *I Love Lucy;* and she hates to cook.

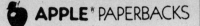